THE STARS AND THE STAGE

D. N. BRYN

The STARS and the STAGE

Guides for Dating Vampires and
Bound by Bound
A Novella

D.N. BRYN

Copyright © 2023 by D. N. Bryn

All rights reserved. This book or any portion thereof may not be reproduced or used in any manner whatsoever without the express written permission of the publisher except for the use of brief quotations in a book review.

Printed in the United States of America
First Printing, 2023

Print (paperback) 978-1-958051-55-9
Print (hardback) 978-1-958051-54-2
Ebook ASIN B0C1W3BR44

For information about purchasing and permissions, contact D.N. Bryn at dnbryn@gmail.com

www.DNBryn.com

Cover design by Covers by Jules

This work is fictitious and any resemblance to real life persons or places is purely coincidental. No vampires were harmed in the making of this story.

This book contains mature content, including the use of blades to consensually open a vein, light masochism during sexual intimacy, and descriptions of past depression.

See the back of the book for a full list.

To us lords and princes,
with our binders and top scars.

We kneel for no one.

1

Diego Figueroa was no princess.

Despite all the times they'd played the part, as glittering homecoming royalty and swishing bridesmaids, as Cinderella and Juliette and Giselle, those roles had never been more than costumes. Standing before their full-length mirror in the Celestial Club's dressing room, wearing a costume that finally fit, that fact was clear. They flashed their fangs and gave a heel-turn, watching the long, loose flaps of their dark suit sparkle with silver as they twirled to the radio's top ten. It was as if they had stepped out of the pages of a fairytale, half elven lord, half gothic rogue, all dark blues and twinkling night skies that paired perfectly with the sapphire stones in their ears.

That was what the Celestial Club's decisive mix of theater dramatics and sensual, live-action role play offered people: a fantasy, curated, inoculated and beautified.

The club owner was incredible at transforming

faded and tattered clothes into immaculate outfits with a few alterations and some tender loving care. Serina had worked personally with Diego on this piece, taking measurements around their chest binder, and adjusting the lines to accentuate Diego's shoulders and taper down their hips. They looked long and lean beneath the fabric, as regal as the part they were meant to play in the club's new event series. They could already imagine the faux jewelry that would ornament their androgynous black bob.

Diego gave the outfit one last satisfied hum before shrugging out of the jacket. "It's perfect, Serina! You're a miracle."

No response came from across the cluttered dressing room.

It was easy to lose oneself in the backstage of the Club, with its convoluted dressing and storage rooms of old paper panels, costumes mounted on every rack and shelf, extra props and lights and furniture stacked between. The superfluous number of mirrors, all old or cracked yet utterly beautiful, only served to visually multiply the already chaotic space. Some days when Diego stepped back here, they felt like they'd walked into a dream.

If only they had known ten years ago that this was the life their pain was leading to—one of love and magic and drama, even if the heart-pounding romance from their teenage years had all but dried up.

Diego turned the radio down, cutting off Green Day halfway through a line of *listen to me whine*. Without the music, it seemed strangely quiet.

"Serina?"

The club regularly built off outfits and fabrics compiled from estate sales and business closure buyouts, and last Diego checked, Serina had been preparing to stock their mound of half-folded cop uniforms in a storage room until their blues could be reused in far better ways, but now the pile sat unattended. Damn, where *was* she? Six months ago, they wouldn't have worried, but since the threats started, it was better to be safe than sorry, and better to be sorry than dead.

Diego prepared to call for her again, but as they stepped toward the hall, they caught a rising sound from the club's side entrance: a near-shouting that included something much like their name.

It was not actually their name—not their name *anymore*—and hadn't been since they'd fled San Salud three months away from a high school diploma, with nothing but a backpack, a black eye, and a fresh pair of fangs that marked them as a second-class citizen. But that had been nearly a decade ago. No one in Los Angeles knew where Diego had come from or who they'd been—no one would have asked them to dig up that trauma. All the fangs at the Celestial Club had a past they would rather forget. Homesickness was their disease and this place was the cure.

Their old homes weren't supposed to come *back*, though.

But here was Diego's, speaking their birthname with a ferocity that shuddered down their spine and a tone that ripped through their chest, clawing up the pain and love they had long since buried.

Their heart pounded, as though their dark, vampiric blood was fighting to break free of their veins. Run, their mind screamed, and they didn't know which way it meant: *to* him or *away* from him. Which way was their safety anymore?

Once it had been his arms, clutching them close when they lost a lead role in drama club or holding them back when the nastier kids had insulted them for their heritage—as though many of their ancestors hadn't lived in California longer than any of these preppy white families—with whispers that this wasn't the time, that vengeance would be sweeter if it couldn't be traced back to them. He had been the safe haven who'd helped them paint everything from dicks on the expensive leather of those bullies' sports cars to the elaborate stage sets that only he and Diego truly appreciated. His were the screams that had echoed their own across the school halls and the hands that had pressed them against the lockers with every ravaging kiss, the only person who avidly agreed with them that the highs and lows of their teenage love was a thing the whole world had to play audience to. He had been the boy who never tried to tame their fire, but always managed to stoke it in a better direction.

Then he'd torn that protection down in one terrible night.

Their safety was here now, Diego reminded themself: it was this club that had offered them a job despite the fangs in their mouth and their lack of experience, its owner who'd taken them in for the first few years, and the platonic love they'd discovered in the process.

They could hear Serina at the door, replying as calmly as her name implied. "I'm sorry, but as I've told you, there's no one here by that name."

Diego numbly wrapped a dark gown over their outfit's brilliant shimmering and slipped down the hallway. As the darkness took over, their vampiric vision shifted to monochrome.

"Please." His voice was strained and pleading, deeper and smoother than it had been. And worn. Like he'd aged from a preppy high school theatre kid into the weathered, silver-tongued prince who'd seen the war and come home a pacifist. Or maybe that was just Diego projecting. "Just tell her that Maddy's here. Tell her I'm sorry."

Diego might have cringed from the accidental misgendering, if not for the swell of other emotions crashing through them at the private nickname Maddox had allowed only for them.

"Maddox? What's that supposed to be—*rugged and pretentious? Did your mom just* know *you'd grow up to be a fancy motorcycle boy, or did you do that to fuck with her?*"

"*Hey, at least I'm not a tiny, spiteful gremlin like you.*" He'd only laughed when they'd smeared their ice cream on his cheek. "*What would you call me, then?*"

"*Maddy,*" they'd hummed. "*Sweet, but wild. And mine.*"

Their Maddy.

After all these years, somehow he'd found them, and he was *sorry*.

The anger that rushed forth shocked Diego—how dare Maddox be sorry, ten years too late, now that Diego had finally beaten back the darkness, reshaped their life into something they genuinely loved, and patched their heart back up until it felt nearly whole again. Whole, but for the shape of *him*.

And *he* was *sorry*.

"Please," Maddox repeated, "I just need her to know."

Diego slipped around the bend in the hall, keeping

to the shadows. They had to see him, if only once more. They could handle that much. They thought they could, at least, until he came into view, and their heart stopped.

Their Maddy was as beautiful as ever, tall and angular, his deep brown waves mussed and his motorcycle helmet tucked under one arm, a leather riding jacket over his other. The angle of the lamp above doorway hid his eyes, but Diego remembered their delicate curvature like the back of their own hand. They could almost hear all the times Maddox had joked that his monolids and his love for a well-tailored suit were the only thing his father had left behind during the business trip that had unwittingly produced him. Diego had always told him that it was a perfect combination, that he was exactly who he should be. That he was the most handsome boy in California.

"Just California?" He'd laughed.

Diego had shoved him playfully. "I don't want you to get a big head. That would throw off your perfect proportions."

"Hmph. Well, I will love you with any size head. I'm just that selfless."

Diego was pretty sure Maddox had kissed them then, tongue roving past their then-flat teeth. He'd love them with any sized head, perhaps, but not with fangs.

As Maddox's gaze wandered over the darkness where Diego stood, he seemed to sense their presence.

"Please."

Serina shook her head. Her grip tightened on the door. "As I've said, there's no one here—"

Diego wasn't sure why they did it, but they stepped forward like a thread had gone taut between them and Maddox. As the light hit them, they almost recoiled, but they forced their chin high. They were no princess. They were the sovereign. Maddox would know just how high they'd risen without him. "The person you're looking for was a myth. When everyone else had shunned me, I found myself."

Serina's confusion turned quickly to understanding. She nodded in a quiet signal of protection.

Maddox met Diego's gaze, but his contemplation didn't hold there, drifting over their androgynous haircut, their flat chest, their small hips. When they'd first found their identity a full year after leaving San Salud, in the midst of what was otherwise their worst days, Diego had secretly wondered how it might feel to be seen as themself by the person who'd once known them best. They had never imagined the way Maddox's attention would consume them, like he was trying to create a hundred memories out of this one moment. "You look… good," he breathed, then seemed to come back to himself with a start. "I—I'm happy for you." His weight shifted and he held out a hand like he meant to surrender something. "And I'd like to apologize."

Apologize. He had said he was sorry, echoed it down the halls, but what good was a word after so long? Diego didn't even know the man who offered it. He was nothing to them.

And they were everything now.

"You're ten years too late for that, Maddy." Diego shook their head. This was all he deserved of them. They took one step back, into the dark, then another.

"Please," Maddox called after them, "at least tell me your name. So I can think of you in terms you approve of."

Diego huffed. "Perhaps I don't want you thinking of me at all." But that was a lie. They wanted Maddox to think of them as much as they had thought of him all these years. To yearn with no release. He deserved that. "Diego," they said, sharply. "My name is Diego now."

"And your pronouns?"

Diego smiled from the shadows. "*They* for my friends, *he* for my lovers."

Maddox watched, and smooth as silk he asked, "Which would I be?"

The way Diego's heart fluttered was all too traitorous. "You get to figure that one out yourself."

With that, they turned their back on him.

Serina spoke with Maddox for so long that Diego nearly went to check on her, but then she returned and the night settled back to normal. She didn't ask Diego questions, and Diego offered no answers. By the time they locked up for the night, it seemed the incident had barely happened. But Diego could not forget it.

On their walk home, they risked sliding on their headphones and starting up their CD player, but they couldn't focus on the music, not when every engine whine made them think of the sleek black Honda Shadow motorcycle Maddox had just gotten for his birthday the year everything fell apart. He'd threatened to buy Diego one of their own—a graduation present, he'd claimed. Graduating class of '84. It felt like a lifetime ago.

It also felt like yesterday, like they'd just lived every touch, every laugh, every theater production and wild night at the boardwalk's roller rink that ended in breathless moans in Maddox's boathouse, the lake bobbing them to sleep in each other's arms after. If only that was all their relationship had been: a blaze that had sizzled out like so many relationships did as they neared college. But they'd chosen to live like they were Romeo and Juliet, so they'd died that way too.

Every brilliant memory was tainted now by the shock of their final meeting as teens, electric like a death sentence. *"What the fuck,"* Maddox had shouted, his voice trembling like he was the one about to sob, and not Diego. *"How could you do this to yourself?"*

"I didn't mean to—I was just trying to help them." The freshly grown fangs in Diego's mouth had still felt wrong, each word a little sloppy. A little salty. They'd learned much later that it was the combination of blood loss and healing vampire venom and bad luck that turned them, but after days of agony as their body had rewritten itself into something new, all they wanted was their boyfriend's arms around them, the promise that they were still loved. All they received was disgust. *"They were going to die without blood."*

"Don't they have places for that?"

"Not for people like—"

Like us, Diego hadn't said. They hadn't known they were trans or queer yet, and even if Maddox had already admitted, quietly, that sometimes he found boys of a more feminine persuasion attractive, he'd never put a label to that, hadn't tried to claim any space in a community where its men were dying and their president seemed content to ignore it so long as it only killed *the gays.*

"Like them," Diego had finished.

Now Diego *was* them—a queer and a vampire— living in a world where one of those things had been nearly killed off by a plague, and humans were doing their best to starve the other to extinction. Humans like the teenager Maddox had been, his fingers curling with revulsion, as though he'd known even then that he was about to ruin their life.

Ten fucking years, he'd waited. Ten fucking years.

Diego had let him go for good reason. He could speak all the pretty words he wanted, but he'd burned their trust with his actions.

If he thought he would earn it back through mere apologies, he was wrong.

2

Diego stood before their dressing room mirror again, their starry outfit donned and their hair nearly finished. With the first session of their new power-dynamic dinner event series starting in half an hour, the backstage areas were a vibrant, bustling mess, nothing like the awkward Tuesday evening when Maddox had knocked on the club's side door last week.

"How many are we expecting will claim my fangs tonight?" Diego asked as Serina slid their final strand of gems into place, the faux sapphires and diamonds glittering like the real things across Diego's hair.

Serina looked just as impeccable, her black curls straightened and pulled up into a feathery bun and the cornrows on her scalp fixed with tiny detachable beads for the night. With so many managerial tasks on her plate, she no longer acted in the events herself, but she always dressed up to match. No one else knew as well as her when to step in if a client got out of hand, or a couple lost their sense of the game, or someone just needed a little encouragement to take their first step.

Serina hummed. "We had seven human singles RSVPed, but I left space for a few more walk-ins. And you never know who might fall head over heels for you, leave their own set of fangs gaping behind them as they pledge you eternal love," she teased, giving Diego's shoulder a squeeze. "You're going to knock them dead."

"I hope not." Diego's lips quirked. "We wouldn't get very far without recurring customers."

Serina laughed.

Diego stared at the mirror long after she moved on. A soft, anxious buzz lingered beneath their skin. They forced themself to breathe in, then out again. They'd played plenty of lead roles as of late, progressing from side characters to one-on-one partners for a human who didn't have a vampire of their own to act through the game with and, finally, to the guiding force of the event. But in the past, they'd still known ahead of time who they'd be paired up with. Tonight they would have to choose in the moment, while making that choice believable.

And, while they tried not to let it, Maddox's appearance had shaken Diego to the roots of their fangs.

Everything they'd worked so hard to heal had been scraped raw again with a single apology. One glance had burned his young cruelty back into them. It was far easier for Diego to work a job where they offered their bite—their lips and their venom and the light, sensual touches that came with—to paying customers when their mind wasn't suddenly crawling with the way Maddox had looked at their fangs the night he'd first seen them. The disgust, the hatred, the terror. Or how not a trace of those emotions had remained when he'd stood beyond the club's door on Tuesday.

Diego shook their head. That meant nothing. Sure, he'd apologized, and maybe he'd grown enough to no longer see their vampirism as a monstrosity, but that was the bare minimum any human *could* do, and tonight Diego would be surrounded by those who saw what they were as a blessing, not a curse. Tonight, Diego Figueroa would reign, the vampire lord of Celestia, in search of their esteemed prey. And their beautiful, terrible Maddy would be nowhere in sight.

The Celestial Club was a place of magic.

Not real magic, of course—science and study had proven that the legendary mythos of immortal vampires who cloaked themselves in darkness and werewolves who transformed into majestic animals were wild overstatements. But for all that their society had accomplished in the twentieth century, people still wanted something to enchant them, to take their breath away. That was what the club offered, from the players to the stage, the crown to the stars.

Serina had transformed the massive warehouse space inch by inch, constructing a labyrinth of wood, paper, and glass walls, twinkling lights erected above with such precision that at a glance it looked real, shining down brighter and fuller than the smog and light-polluted LA night sky had in decades. From room to room, event to event, the club would shift: a fantastical medieval throne, or a Victorian ball, or a crumbling gothic castle with blood-red table clothes and flickering candles, all centralized around the small, cushioned chambers where guests could escape for more private fun. Years ago, Diego had been drawn by the pay bump that came with attending those secluded engagements, but they'd quickly found that it wasn't their preferred form of acting. They were made for a wider audience.

Tonight would be their largest yet.

This event's main space was one of the more fantastical: a gothic dining hall turned as salaciously starry as the club's name, with glimmering deep blue spreads over the long tables that ran on three sides, the central floor empty beneath the warehouse's fictional night sky. More twinkling lights were scattered between crystal dishware. Glittering silver shone from the sheer drapes that swathed walls and chairs and couches, the whole scene abounding with gold accents, dark velvet and white lilies.

It was glorious. And for the next three weeks, it was Diego's.

They could already hear the little crowd of forty or so guests gathering in the central event space, each attendee's entrance announced with their selected title. Most were couples of vampires and humans, though some came in larger partnered groups or as singles paying extra for an actor to pair with them for the event. The club's events ranged from casual solitary nights to month-long sessions where the most dedicated might attend nearly all of the five open days a week, and while some catered towards specific power imbalances—most commonly vampires whose humans played as blood slaves—this particular one had been designed for a lighter, less restricted style of dominance, with intensified chivalry and tests of love. Like the one Diego was meant to use to select their event partner.

"You ready?" the platonic love of Diego's life asked, flashing his fangs.

Valentine's serving outfit hid just how important he'd be for the event, charged with helping Diego monitor and maintain the game's thrilling but safe atmosphere as he carried out Diego's commands. If anything went terribly wrong, the slim sword at his hip was far from pretend. He held Diego's crown metaphorically, just as much as he did literally, cradling the silver circlet between his gloved fingertips. It had been like that since the moment they'd first arrived at the club, two months apart, Diego all rage and Valentine a flighty, uncertain mess, three years younger but already far more experienced in the prejudices against his vampirism. They had taken to each other like long-lost family, vowing a bond stronger than blood. Diego's heart still yearned for the drama and fire of a romantic relationship, but if Valentine was the only partner the universe ever saw fit to give them, his love would be enough.

There was no one else Diego would rather have had at their side, in life or in the theater.

They smirked, straightening their shoulders. "I was born for this."

It didn't matter that it was a clichéd quote, it was the truth. As Valentine lowered their silver circlet onto their jewel-strewn head, Diego felt the world shift to accommodate. Tonight, they were all powerful. Invincible. Nothing Maddox Burke had done, or could ever do, would hurt them.

Diego stepped out of the veiled backstage to the majestic dimming of the lights. The crowd quieted reverently, as though Diego truly was their esteemed sovereign, finally descending into their midst.

"Good evening, my dear guests…" Diego kept an edge to their lofty tone. They did not want to come off as cruel, but merely hints of sinister: a creature both beautiful and threatening.

The guests in question bowed and curtseyed.

Diego walked among them, eyes roving and lips quirked. They paused before a vampire in a deep plum dress, her rented jewels gleaming in the candlelight. "Lady Lissette."

Many of the guests attended under fictional names, and Diego knew those who weren't regulars by the photos they'd submitted, along with a survey of preferences and character stories that the club could use to shape their experience to best suit them. Lissette smiled politely, and the human on her arm bowed his head.

Diego turned their attention to him. "And who is this?" They added a slight purr to the line, which made Lissette's real-life husband, Henry, flush nearly as red as his hair.

Lissette petted his fingers, possessively. "Pretty, isn't he?"

"He certainly smells lovely." Diego leaned in, breathing against Henry's neck. The way his gaze snapped to Lissette's fangs told Diego they were playing the scene just right. They stepped back with a huff. "But is he worthy of you? How deep does his desire run?"

"My dedication to my lady is endless," Henry replied, not taking his eyes off Lissette.

Diego made an unsatisfied sound and smiled, just a little wicked. "Perhaps later we'll make you prove that."

They moved on to the sapphic couple a few paces down. Countess Amile perched on the edge of the table, holding her vampiric lover possessively as she chatted with the person beside her. Each time Amile nudged against her lover's lips, the vampire would open her mouth and let her partner prick her finger, receiving a dose of blissful vampiric venom before Amile withdrew to press the cut to a white handkerchief.

Diego hadn't found someone they'd felt comfortable playing that docile a role with—to give venom without receiving any blood, offering their fangs so intimately to another person and expecting nothing in return still terrified them—but this vampire, whose stage name she'd written only as *Amile's*, seemed utterly content with it… and just as content with the way her human lover's hand was clearly fiddling beneath her dress.

"Are you keeping her fangs sharp, Countess?" Diego teased, and when Amile nudged her vampire's mouth back open to show them off, Diego dared a soft touch to one of them.

That was the beauty of this event, they thought— that whatever dynamics were acted out, every vampire's fangs were treated as something special and important.

Not monstrous, not disgraceful, but beautiful. They bared their own, and Amile beamed in response.

Diego moved throughout the room, engaging with the guests who desired it and exchanging simple nods with the ones who had marked themselves as uninterested. Each time they passed one of the humans who'd come without a partner, they made a show of eyeing the person over: a lick of the lips, a kiss on the hand, a finger to the pulse. In some places, androgyny such as theirs was seen as deviant, but here it was desirable—this lord of the vampires could be anyone's fantasy. Soon though, Diego would have to choose who would get to be claimed by them for the next three weeks.

The young woman in the black dress could make a fine choice for a femme fatale working her way to the top through mysterious means, or perhaps the silver fox with his elegant cane could be Diego's by right of his age. Or they could fluster everyone by choosing one of the two humans dating Duke Quincy.

The little head table that overlooked the room had two chairs already behind it, two place settings, and one circlet of gems, deep blue and sparkling. Mine, the circlet said. Claimed.

Diego made a show of fingering it as they passed, giving time for the guests to mingle around the edges of the room, wine flowing and chatter rising and falling, little storylines playing out simultaneously. Valentine slipped up beside Diego. They could barely hear him beneath the jovial voices and low orchestral music.

"We have a latecomer. He'll burst through the front once you make your announcement."

"A human?"

"Yes."

That could change things. Another piece on the board—one Diego would be expected to put more weight on due to the dramatics of the situation. Usually special entrances like this were bestowed by Serina on more experienced guests; Diego would have to trust that their boss knew what she was doing. "Well, let's get this party started then, shall we?"

Valentine smiled.

As he backed away, Diego stepped toward the guests, raising their voice enough that the hidden mic on their collar would carry their proclamation to the far sides of the room. "It may have come to your attention that my last human consort has recently… disappointed me." They let the vague statement linger, allowing the guests to draw their own conclusions. "This opens a place at my side: coveted; esteemed. Be warned though, those who strive to claim it must prove themselves beyond a doubt. I will not see the mistakes of my previous partner repeated. If you want to be the one blessed with my fangs, you will have to bare your throat." They let their gaze drift from human to human, lingering on those who'd marked themselves as interested in participation. Their lips twisted, not in threat but in challenge, and they bared their teeth, letting their tongue grace the fangs they were offering up, a drop of their intoxicating venom already pooling at the tips. "Are there even any here worthy of such an honor? Announce yourself, if you wish to claim the place of my consort, and we'll discover whether or not I find you wanting."

Excited murmurs came from the shifting crowd. The woman in the black dress was the first to move, followed quickly by three others, but none of them had a chance to voice their intentions before the disruption. Even knowing it was coming, Diego flinched as the double entrance doors were heaved open, their heart giving a little jump. Then, it seemed to stop beating entirely.

Standing in the entrance, one hand still clutched to the edge of each door, was Maddox.

He wore a fantastical array of stormy blues, his half tunic pinned to one shoulder by a golden brooch, and a fitted suit beneath, his elegant black leather motorcycle boots blending seamlessly into the costume. The draping line of sapphire lookalikes in his hair seemed picked precisely to match with Diego's, and his intentions could not have been clearer than the heat of his gaze. He fixed his attention on Diego like they were his only reason to exist. "Take me as your consort, my lord."

Diego's lungs tightened against the burning of their chest. Their world tunneled to just Maddy as he strode into the room, across the cleared central space, each step the sound of a war drum. He was here, in Diego's space, in Diego's *home*.

And everyone was watching, expectant.

"Prince Maddox of the Grave Gate." They sneered, throwing in the latter half of the title as a reference to San Salud's famous cemeteries. They paced as they spoke, like this was all part of the scene. Like it wasn't threatening to destroy them. "Have you forgotten how you last betrayed me when I came to your kingdom? How you took our love and threw it on the pyre?"

"I have not forgotten," Maddox replied. "Not for a day nor an hour." He had always been lithe, but he came to a halt with the grace of a panther, and in a dramatic, sweeping motion he dropped to his knee, the drapes of his outfit flaring around him. "And I return to you to beg your forgiveness. I submit my life unto you; take me if you wish or discard me if it suits you."

Another apology.

Diego felt this one like the kiss of a flame, no pain left, only anger, sharp and harsh and fueled by every moment they'd spent together: the long hours in the theater room, leaning against each other as they worked through lines that their high school's audience would never appreciate, rocks thrown at each other's windows until one night Diego's had cracked, lounging together at the lake on long summer days, laughing about bad poetry, and racing, disgusting and sunburnt, to the arcade after to drink vodka from soda cups and fight over the Pac-Man machine.

They were children's sentiments from an era Diego wouldn't have returned to even if they could. But they should have been happy, lighthearted memories. The man standing before them had changed that.

Diego could feel Valentine's presence at their back, waiting and watching, judging how to move forward with this new act Diego had thrown the event into. With all the speed and agility their vampirism granted, Diego drew the blade from within Valentine's sheath. They pointed it casually at Maddox, and strode forward, one perfectly placed step at a time.

Maddox continued to kneel. He bowed his head, but his gaze did not leave Diego, hot and fierce and utterly infuriating.

Diego slipped the tip of the sword beneath his chin. They lifted. The room went deadly quiet as Maddox swallowed against the metal. Slowly, he bared his throat to Diego.

At this distance, only a sword length between them,

Diego caught his familiar scent, the oaky musk deeper and fuller than last time they'd been this close. He'd held pliers in his sweaty, shaking hands then, his voice cracking on every word: *"Maybe if you pull them out."*

It hadn't mattered that vampires could retract their fangs at will, that Diego was still mostly the same as they had been, just with a garlic allergy, an inability to stand the sun, and a necessity for blood. When they'd shoved him away, their new strength had sent him crashing through the shelves at his back with a disturbing thud. They'd been too hungry not to immediately fixate on the scent of his blood on the wood.

"Fuck—I didn't mean to do that," they'd managed to say, and *"I can help,"* fangs baring in the knowledge that their mouth could heal just as much as it could hurt.

But Maddox had fled all the same, screaming at them like they were the monster. For nearly two years after, they'd believed they were, believed their tragic life was worth so little that they'd found a painful solace in the thought of ending it. Only this place—its insistence that they were loved, desired, valued—had finally brought back their self-confidence. They had a role to fill here tonight, a fiction to keep putting on.

But Diego didn't feel like acting anymore. They felt like driving in the point of their blade, waiting for the pain to spill across Maddox's face, for him to know the betrayal they had suffered ten years ago. But they suspected that would hurt them both just as much.

If Maddox had signed up for this event though, donned a costume and everything, that meant he knew the safe words. Diego could push him. They could push him, and eventually he'd break. Then he'd leave, for good this time, and give Diego's heart the space to heal all over again.

They pushed the sword blade just a little harder, a little deeper, and tugged a hair upward.

The room gasped.

Maddox's shock and fear was delicious for the full moment it lasted, before the shame hit Diego and they withdrew the sword in a dramatic swoop. Maddox gingerly fingered the shallow cut that now dragged beneath the point of his chin. It came away red. The mere sight of it mesmerized Diego, like his absence from their life had given their soul ten years to carve him a bigger space in it, to hone every sense to his being.

This had been a mistake.

Somehow Maddox himself was making it worse by not flinching away from Diego's obvious craving, by leaning in where ten years ago he'd jerked back, screaming as he fled. This time, he held his bloodied finger out, a soft expression on his face. "Would you accept a taste, my lord?"

Diego snorted, trying to cover up their yearning. Too little, too late. "Your blood is fit only for the gutter rats."

"My lord, give him a chance," Lissette called, and a little purr came into her voice as she added, "Or I might."

That got a laugh from the crowd, not easing the tension but rather turning it electric.

The silver fox shouted, "Yes, let him prove himself."

"Do your worst, we'll see if he can take it," another human echoed.

They were right, of course. As much as Diego wanted to turn Maddox out, the *vampire lord* immediately kicking such a willing human contestant from the game wouldn't go over well—especially after Diego had just fabricated them an elaborate history. No one else here could know it was all mostly real. No one but Serina, anyway. Fuck, Diego would have to chat with her later.

They turned, slowly, drawing one finger along the blade of their borrowed sword. "I suppose I have to play by my own rules." They bared their fangs, watching for even a hint of hesitation from their long-lost betrayer. "Do you accept my challenges, Prince Maddox?"

"I do," Maddox breathed.

Diego smiled, sharp as the weapon in their hands. "Then strip."

3

Diego had never seen their crowd so singularly engaged. The club liked to provide the outline of a story for those too intimidated or inexperienced to form their own, but at its core their events were about providing a space for people to play out their personal fantasies. Tonight, though, as Maddox rose to his feet and stoically unpinned his outer cloak, the room was enthralled with him and with each step Diego took as they circled like a predator.

Maddox obediently folded his cloak and handed it to a waiting Valentine, then shrugged out of his suit jacket. As his undershirt followed, Diego's lungs caught. They tried not to stare, not to follow the lines of every toned muscle. This was their Maddy, yet he was a brand-new canvas too, their skinny theater boy's bony limbs now thick and solid, his abs defined, with a trail of dark hair that snaked beneath his pant line in a way that made Diego wonder, absently, what else might have changed.

Atop the musculature, his skin bore new marks. The

few light blemishes might have been recently healed scrapes. A tattoo of an inverted crown dripped black blood down his ribs. Just behind his left shoulder lay a mangled scar. Diego knew that one. Their fingers moved without consent, touching it so lightly that Maddox visibly shivered.

Diego pulled back. "I see your flesh still remembers where I stabbed you."

"I was the cause of that," Maddox retorted, sure and fast. "You were never to blame, my lord."

His confidence felt like a physical object that curled between Diego's ribs and toyed with their heart.

Maddox unfastened his boots, his shoulder muscles flexing as he pulled them off, and peeled away his socks after. Slowly, he undid his belt. His hands went to the rim of his pants. The murmurs of the crowd reached a crescendo, before going silent to the gentle swish of his pants falling free of his lean, muscled legs. The boxers he wore underneath were silky as satin and twice as revealing, cradling fluidly around a package that looked like it had grown to fit the rest of him. Diego had to fight to tear their gaze from it.

They had both been relatively shameless in their youth—the whole school knew when they were fighting, when they were fucking, sometimes *how* and *where* they were fucking too, and in the process seen nearly as much of them as they'd seen of each other—but as Maddox hooked one thumb under the elastic of his underwear, his attention fixing on Diego like a blazing inferno, something hot and tight within them panicked.

They stopped him with a sharp smile. "That will be sufficient."

"For the moment anyway," Lissette muttered. Her husband looked like he agreed.

"What would you have of me next?" Maddox's voice was low and sultry, and while he stood there in nothing but his silky undergarment before all of Diego's court, he acted as though they were the only two people in the room.

Diego would change that. "I'll have your veins. And bring me a glass, Valentine… a glass for every vampire here, and anyone else who would like a taste of him."

Maddox didn't waiver. He held his arm out, watching Diego with a steady surety as they lifted their borrowed sword. They held the hilt in one hand and rested the blade between two fingers of their other to steady it as they carefully lowered it to the vein on the underside of Maddox's wrist. They pressed down, watching as his skin tensed, then split. His blood spilled in a red rivulet across his wrist, the delicious scent of it wafting on the air, dusky and dry.

Diego fought the urge to lift the vein to their mouth and instead slipped one of the shot-sized crystal glasses Valentine offered under the stream. As it filled, the red darkened. Valentine helped them switch out the receptacle, holding the next in their place.

Diego approached Lissette. They held the first cup out to her with a flare of dramatics. "Drink of him and tell me whether his feigned loyalty is worth my trouble."

Lissette lifted the glass to her lips. Her eyes closed, and she hummed with the kind of sincere delight that meant she could clearly smell what Diego did in Maddox's blood. She drained the glass. "He tastes as exquisite as his extraordinary deference."

The next vampire emerged behind her, followed quickly by another, each taking a long sip of their own cup before making some proclamation, whether to the taste or to Maddox's honor or his past betrayal. All the while, Diego could feel Maddox's attention fixed on them. It no longer burned, just warmed, soft and constant.

But Diego could see the toll that losing that much blood was taking on him. They swore they could hear his heart rate increase, and by the time they were through half their vampiric guests, he was blinking just to keep his focus on Diego steady.

"You grow weary already," Diego taunted, but it felt a little cruel in their mouth. They reminded themself that he knew the safe words just the same as the rest of them, an easy way out if this grew too much. He was here of his own volition. If he suffered, that was his choice too.

Maddox took a deep breath and seemed to hold himself in place. "My heart may give out but so long as there's a chance I might regain your trust, I will persist."

"So be it," Diego grumbled.

From out of the backstage, someone—probably Serina—produced a chair, and Valentine helped Maddox into it. Maddox squeezed his hand in thanks after, an act so strangely considerate that it disquieted Diego. If they hadn't known Valentine's preferences—or lack thereof—they'd have thought he looked flustered by it. His previously professional attention turned gentler. Diego wanted to tell him to stop, to not risk his own heart the way they had.

Maddox continued to bleed.

The whole room smelled of him now, the appetizing scent impossible to retreat from no matter how many circles Diego strode. They continued to watch him. He stared back, his face paled by the cupfuls spilled from his wrist. Diego tried not to worry. They didn't know when their anger had faded, but all they felt now were the knots in their gut and the shallowness of Maddox's breathing.

The next time they passed by him, they drew their hand along his chair and let their long nails absently flutter across his hair where it curled around the nape of his neck. "You can desist, if the challenge is too much.

Return to your own kingdom in shame but alive."

"I would rather bleed out at your feet."

"Then you're a fool," Diego growled, leaning toward his ear, trying not to think of how near they were, of how wonderful he smelled, how the slope of his neck was fuller and stronger than the one they'd littered in kisses so many times as a teen. "Surrender, Prince Maddox." Then softer, they added, "You have a safe word."

He turned his face, his nose an inch from Diego's and his breath hot on their lips. "I won't surrender, not until you accept me, my starlight." The pet name he used was the opposite of a traditional safe word—an acknowledgement of the risks and a request to continue—but Diego could see that the whole statement wasn't a line or an act. It was just the truth, desperation and stubbornness written across his face.

The damn beautiful fool would die here if it came to that.

For Diego.

They felt struck through the heart, like the last ten years had been wiped away and they were watching the door bang closed behind a bleeding Maddox for the last time, not yet knowing it would be the end of them—the end of their relationship and the end of Diego's life in San Salud. And here he'd come back, so strong and sure, willing to bleed for them. He had to have an ulterior motive, some reason why he'd come now, after all this time.

Diego didn't trust him. But they realized they couldn't keep hurting him either. Even if he had deserved it, once, even if a part of Diego still believed he deserved it now, he had laid himself at their feet, and kicking him suddenly felt cruel.

As the last cup filled, Maddox's head began to loll. Diego caught it with a supportive hand to the back of his neck, trying to appear as aloof and skeptical as ever, and lifted his seeping wrist into the air. With the hand over his head, his bleeding slowed, a trickle of red still trailing down his bare arm.

"Let it be known that this is the cost of breaking my trust… and of regaining it."

"Then say that you'll have me." Despite the slur in his voice, Maddox spoke it loud enough for the crowd to hear. His gaze though, was only for Diego.

They swore they could sense the drip-drip of blood from his elbow. It might mean three weeks of him, if they said yes—three weeks that he would sit at their side, expected to sigh beneath their fangs. Three weeks where he could turn around and stab them in the heart again.

"Take him back, my lord," Henry called, and others followed with cries of "He's earned his place" and "Look at him, he's already yours!"

Diego tried not to flinch. They lifted their chin and flashed their fangs at their eager onlookers. "Prince

Maddox has won himself a second chance. But one slip, one lie," they hissed, dropping their gaze back to him, "and I will have you flayed alive and served as a delicacy."

Maddox lifted his head, leaning into their touch, and smiled. "As you wish."

For a moment, Diego felt nothing but tender, warm and wonderful and free. It startled them so much that they pulled back, dropping his arm. Their fingers shook like they'd been burned. "Valentine, finish him off for me. I'm no longer hungry."

Diego forced themself to watch as Valentine carefully licked Maddox's wound to heal it and pressed his fangs into Maddox's skin to inject him with the venom that would increase his blood regeneration process tenfold, again with the extra hint of tenderness that Diego swore was more than mere professionalism. They waited for a grimace from Maddox, some sign that the teenager who'd been so disgusted by their partner's vampiric state that he'd sent them fleeing San Salud was still in there, waiting to show his true colors. But he smiled at Valentine instead, then at Diego, his gaze burning them up.

The rest of the night passed in a blur, Diego moving from one guest to the next, barely pausing long enough to sit beside Maddox for the meal that came with this particular event. Diego had laid the circlet on his head, and Valentine had helped him back into his costume, exchanging soft words that Maddox returned with just as much resolute affection as he'd shown Diego. He'd been dazed for the next few hours as his body fought to renew all the blood he'd spilled for them. After that, he seemed oddly content to watch and smile, conversing in character with anyone who approached and sitting pleasantly by himself with a glass of wine otherwise. His gaze still rarely left Diego.

It was like he was trying to memorize them all over again, redefine who they were in his head.

It left Diego conscious of just how much he'd changed as well—the strong muscles, the unflinching courage. He'd always been dramatic and intense—that was one of the things that had drawn Diego to him in the first place, the way every time their eyes met, Maddox seemed to be having a private conversation with them, like they were reincarnated lovers with centuries of history that no one else could possibly understand. They'd lived like that, too, a pair of hopeless teenagers who'd thought their young love was different from everyone else's, until the moment it had fallen apart.

But then, here he was ten years later, watching Diego with all the same contemplation and fire, so perhaps what they'd had *was* different.

That didn't mean it could work.

When guests asked whether they were going to taste their consort soon, Diego feigned disinterest and irritation, as though they were fighting their craving for the delicious Prince Maddox just to spite him, and not secretly terrified of what biting him might mean for them both. They would have to deal with the consequences of that later, as customers showed up expecting Diego to slowly melt to Maddox's charms and treat him as a coveted prize. But they told themself that by then, Maddox would probably have fled Diego's life with the same speed as last time.

In the wee hours of the morning, guests began exchanging farewells, characters falling away to reveal the tired but happy people beneath. Diego offered them a final sovereign's salutation, deliberately snubbing Prince Maddox of the Grave Gate, and retreated to the backstage with Valentine.

They cornered Serina with such speed that even she looked mildly surprised. She turned from the prop she'd been adjusting with a knowing smile. "Yes?"

"You—" Diego hissed, but their emotions caught in their throat, and too quickly, Valentine cut them off.

"Don't blame Serina, I approved, too." He pressed a

hand to Diego's shoulder, like that was some kind of comfort. Ordinarily it would have been—they valued Valentine's opinion like it was their own, and his love meant the world to them, but goddamn him if he was going to be employing it where *Maddox* was concerned.

They shrugged off his touch, returning it with two middle fingers. "Fuck you both, then."

"We thought it would be nice for you to reconnect," Serina replied, as ever the perfect calm against Diego's fire.

Valentine added, "And you always enjoy a theatrical public apology."

"He's right." Serina lifted a brow as she said it, affectionate but pointed. "You can't air all your dirty laundry during events for years and not expect your family to eventually respond in kind."

"That's not fair," Diego retorted, equally sure that after the hell they'd spent their life stirring in public, it probably actually was.

Valentine sighed, rubbing at his neck. "I'm sorry. It's just so rare that someone comes looking for us wanting to make amends. If it was my past showing up with that much love and devotion, I just figured…"

The pain in his voice cut Diego open. He'd retracted his fangs, they noticed. It had been a long time since he'd done that in the safety of the Celestial Club, but it reminded Diego of when he'd first joined them, the way he'd been too afraid to work with his fangs out, even in the highly vetted and protected environment the club fostered. Back then, he'd hidden other parts of himself as well, capped his emotions behind his naturally stoic expression and his eyes under a mass of blonde bangs he'd finally let Serina trim last year.

He'd taken the first threat on the Celestial Club even harder than she had.

Diego's anger wilted under the shadow of his pain—pain that looked so much like the mirror of their own. "You don't know what he did to me."

Valentine's pale cheeks flushed. He looked away.

Serina held Diego's gaze, though. Gentle, but firm, she said, "I *do* know, Diego. Maddox wouldn't be here otherwise."

A flash of horror slid through Diego, nauseous in their gut. "What did he tell you?"

"That I betrayed your trust and your love in the most painful way possible," Maddox spoke from behind them, stepping slowly into the backstage space. In his regal outfit, he still looked like a prince, but he sounded like Diego's Maddy. "I was stupid and selfish and cruel. But I never meant—" He shook his head. "I told my mother you'd tried to bite me because I was too ashamed to admit that it was my own damned fault I came home sobbing and bleeding. I'd never imagined she'd take it to the police."

Just hearing the words spoken out loud was like reliving the moment from a distance, the flash of the cop car lights, the banging on Diego's door. Their parents' combined horror over learning of their vampirism and the assault allegations in one go had stalled the officers long enough for Diego to sneak out the window. But as bad as that had been, it was the trying to return later that night that had hit them worse. The realization that everyone knew, and they were all, like Maddox, too afraid of Diego's new fangs to listen to anything they had to say.

"Oh god," Valentine whispered, horror clear on his face. "Maybe we should have kicked him out?"

"You think?" Diego snapped, but they shoved their hand through their hair, ripping off the silver circlet. They could not stop watching Maddox—his remorseful expression, the humility of his stance, his determined patience as he stood there—and hearing his apology repeating in their head. "Or no. I mean, fuck."

"I'm sorry I sprung this on you." Serina sounded so damned motherly as she said it. "If his presence here is too painful for you, then he'll leave, no questions. But I have reason to believe he's a good man, or I would never have let him on the premises, and he's far from the only person in this building with a past they regret. We are in the business of handing out second chances, not denying them."

That made Diego feel worse, somehow. While Serina was—at least mostly—human, as a single Black lesbian who openly hired vampires, it had taken her an inexplicable number of tears and labor to reach the place she had, yet never did she let that detract from the care she showed for every person who passed through her doors. People who no one else thought deserved it. But most of those were vampires, acting the way they did because society had given them no other choice. They were not Maddox.

Serina must have understood Diego's hesitation because she lifted one brow at Maddox. "What do *you* have to say for yourself?"

Maddox looked back at her in such a way that made Diego wonder just what they'd spoken of that night he'd arrived backstage—what had possibly made her recommend he come back for this—but then his attention fixed back on Diego, intense and impossible. "Only that, again, I'm sorry. And that what I've done has no bearing on who I am now... or it does," he amended. "It made me someone who bleeds freely because I know there's a young vampire out there somewhere accused of an act they are not to blame for, with no one willing to stand up for them."

"Maddy..." His name slipped from Diego's lips without their consent, and they felt instantly ashamed of the crack in their voice.

Not that Maddox hadn't seen them weep before, hadn't held them while their cramps threatened to make them pass out or praised their compassion when an injustice on the news broke them into angry sobs. But that final time they'd come to him in tears, he'd pulled out pliers and ruined their life with a lie. And now he'd come back to bleed freely. To bleed for *them*.

Diego dragged in a breath. Fuck Serina, fuck Valentine, and *yet*. "Can I have a minute with him? Alone."

"You can use my office," Serina offered.

They walked there in silence, Valentine awkwardly following at a distance, his sword still at his hip. Diego had to smile at him and make a shooing motion to finally get across the point that they'd be safe. *They* were the predator, after all. The sun was hours from rising, and Maddox clearly had no holy silver on him, though from what they'd seen of this new him, Diego found they couldn't imagine him going through the effort to find and purchase such a rare and harmful metal in the first place.

As soon as the door closed behind them, Diego spun on him. "Why are you here?"

He looked just as conflicted as Diego felt. "In LA or at the club?"

"In this room," Diego shouted, "staring at me like that!"

"Because I miss you!" Finally, he shouted back, but where Diego's emotions were all scalding heat, his were warmth and deep desire. "I could never discover where you'd gone after you left San Salud, and I—I figured you preferred that. But then I saw your fangs on a Celestial Club poster at one of the vampire-accepting speakeasies—"

"That was just the lower half of my face," Diego protested. Serina had purposefully cut out enough that the wrong people couldn't identify them. Yet here Maddox was.

"With the tiny mole beneath your lips and that crooked third tooth on the left?" He didn't even glance down as he said it, his gaze fixed on their eyes. "You think I don't still know every line of your mouth, Diego?"

They had to stop from lifting a hand to their own lips. A little shudder ran through them, not entirely unpleasant.

"As soon as I realized that you worked here," he continued, "that I'd finally found you again after so long—I knew I needed to apologize."

"And you did that. So why did you come back tonight? Why have you *stayed*?"

"Because I want us to have another chance."

Another chance, after ten years? Even after all Diego had witnessed, it felt impossible. "I've changed, Maddy,

I'm a different person now."

"And you think I haven't changed, too?" Maddox stepped toward them—had he always been this tall?—and they could see the gleam along his lower lids as he clutched a hand over his heart. "Every cell in my body has died since I knew you. There's not an inch of me that you've touched anymore. I am, entirely, a new being. And yet I still love you."

I still love you. Diego's chest hurt, as though their heart could bleed from emotional wounds alone. They wanted to snap back that it didn't matter, because *they* no longer loved *him*. They'd moved on. He should too. But it would be a lie. They could not possibly feel this much pain and anger and longing if they didn't still have feelings for him.

Indifference, not hate, was the opposite of love, and Diego was anything but indifferent towards Maddox.

"Oh, fuck you." They gave his chest a little push, their vampiric strength held easily in check after so many years adjusting to it.

He smiled, barely wobbling, and caught their hand. "Well, I see you haven't changed *that* much."

Diego nearly yanked back out of spite, but Maddox let them go before they could. The moment they lost contact, something in them wanted it back—wanted to touch every one of his new cells, discover the way each felt all over again. Instead they snorted, giving their fingers a little shake. "I *have* touched a few inches of you now."

He traced the places that Diego's skin had brushed his over the course of the night. "Thank you for that. And for this night, for giving me a chance."

"Yeah, well, it was the least I could do. Literally. The events have a whole list of rules everyone has to abide by."

"I read them—the customer ones, anyway. I think Serina added to my agreement on purpose, to protect you. She seems to care about you a lot. You deserve that. You've *always* deserved that."

That seemed to break the tension between them for the first time since Diego had locked eyes with Maddox at the side door of the club. They sighed, setting their crown on Serina's desk and boosting themselves onto it. "So, I guess this is where I ask you how you've been?"

"Is it?" Maddox chuckled. "I wouldn't know. My script ended here."

"Well that's just sloppy writing."

"I know? I should talk to the director." He leaned against the wall, loosening from his shoulders to his smile, though the intensity of his gaze remained constant. "I've been all right. Graduated college with a double major in psychology and history, neither of which I'll ever use, took a television acting gig until my soul started sliding out through my ass, and since then

I've just been... finding myself?"

"And going to the gym." Diego motioned with their chin, salaciously scanning his new musculature. Maddox laughed, and he returned the favor with such a mix of heat and dramatics that Diego could not even reproach him despite the flush it brought on. That made them wonder if Maddox had noticed just how much their skin had lightened without regular sunlight to bring out the natural melanin. Whether that obvious vampiric quality bothered him.

But no other part of their vampirism seemed to bother him anymore. "And you?" he asked. "You've been doing well, if your performance tonight was anything to go by. This seems like an amazing place."

"It's certainly not prime time television." Diego wasn't embarrassed to work in a field that catered to kink, but it was still nice to know that Maddox wouldn't judge them for it. Not that they'd feared that, particularly, after the show *he'd* put on earlier. "I do love it. This kind of acting provides so much freedom, and it's really only half presentation—the other half is reading the audience, finding ways to engage them and help free *them* to live out their own fantasies, so they can find the same joy in the performing that I have." And it meant that sometimes Diego got to live out their own fantasies while they did. Fantasies like torturing their ex-boyfriend when he came to apologize ten years too late.

Not that he had ever actually been tortured by their demands, if the expression he wore while reminiscing was anything to go by. "You do an incredible job. I was so stressed when I first arrived because, I mean, you could have chosen not to allow my frankly kind of childish fancies and kicked me out—but that was still the most fun I've had in a long time."

"I made you strip and drained you until you nearly passed out. Fuck, what is your life *like* now?"

"Not particularly pleasurable, I'll admit." He laughed, and his eyes left theirs for a split second, before coming back. "But besides the blood loss—which, technically, I don't mind—the way we fed off each other, and the other guests played along, and everyone got so into it, but it was all safe and open and oddly honest despite the acting? I haven't felt that in years. Not since I was last with you." His voice lowered, still possessing all the determination of Prince Maddox but with a soft, pleading edge that was purely Maddy. "Please, I know I'm a broken record at this point, but give me another chance. I won't expect anything from you, and you can banish me at any time. I still love you, Diego, and I want to see if that love is capable of changing to fit the new us."

Diego's heart stuttered. They crossed their arms against the sensation. "When you showed up at the club last week, did you think you were going to win me back?"

His lips didn't twitch up but he seemed to smile all the same, staring at them like he could see into their soul. "I didn't have plans for that yet. I just knew that if I could reach you finally, I needed to apologize. But then you were glorious, so how could I not fight for you?"

"I'm also still a tiny, spiteful gremlin," Diego muttered, because Maddox calling them glorious while staring at them like he believed it was suddenly far too much.

"Oh, yes, was I not clear? The thing I find glorious is that you *are* a tiny, spiteful gremlin."

"Fuck off." But this time Diego was laughing, their cheeks burning with another blush. Ah, fuck him. Fuck how their heart still hurt from his betrayal and fuck how it ached for more of this all the same. "One chance, Maddy," they said. "For now, I'll allow you to visit me during events, prove that you mean what you're saying, and then we'll see. But if you break my heart again, I'll do far more than flay you alive."

"My lord, I will accept your worst and still I'll not dream of hurting you." He looked so sincerely like he meant it.

Then the brick came hurling at Diego through Serina's office window.

It missed them both by a few inches, crashing into

the far end of the desk and thudding to the ground in front of Maddox.

"Fuck." Diego launched toward the window, ignoring the crunch of glass beneath their feet as they struggled to spot whoever had thrown the projectile. Even with their night vision, it was too bright inside and too dark beyond to make out the fleeing human. But Diego knew who the culprit had to be—the same people who'd been sending the club threats for months now.

This wasn't just a threat, though. It was an escalation. And so long as the police were willing to turn a blind eye toward acts of violence against establishments that hired vampires—and step in *against* the victims if push came to shove—things would likely keep escalating.

Maddox knelt over the brick, carefully unwrapping a paper rubber-banded to the side. He didn't look shaken or scared, only darkly thoughtful as he spread it open for Diego.

Serina Freeman, you've ignored our demands
for too long. Keep supporting the monsters
of our city, and we will see that your
establishment supports no one ever again.
— LA's Paladins

4

INTERLUDE

Maddox Burke was no prince.

For all his pleasantries and gallantry, there was grime on his boots and blood on his hands. Some part of him thought maybe it had always been there, even before this turn of fate—before his life had become vampire fangs and threats hurled with enough force to kill.

He could not stop thinking about that brick as he sped through the quiet 3am street, the reverberation of his motorcycle echoing beneath the lamps. A foot to the left, and Diego would have been hit. *Diego,* his Diego.

"They to my friends, he to my lovers."

Maddox still didn't know which he was—whether he deserved to be called either. He couldn't think of Diego anyway, not without his heart aching and all his emotions tangling into a mess of want and joy and terror and guilt.

But he *could* think about that brick.

He was pretty sure whoever threw it hadn't seen him. He'd been too close to the wall, shadowed by Serina's large bookshelf. He supposed he'd find out either way, and besides, there was nothing he could do about it now. The Paladins had made their decision, and while they had, he'd been lounging in the vampire's lair.

Discovery wasn't the only thing he feared, though. This violence came too soon; he hadn't expected such an immediate escalation.

Maddox needed more time—more time with Diego. And whatever it took, he was going to get it.

5

The show had to go on.

It was a truth as much as a cliché—the Celestial Club had accepted their customer's payments for the current event and they couldn't afford to return them based on a threat bound to a single brick. Instead, they took precautions, keeping the front doors locked and instructing customers to come through the side entrance with their hoods up and faces covered. So far, nothing more had happened.

But Diego was sure it would only be a matter of time.

The club was host to plenty of other tension that month, too, with Maddox appearing promptly every night. He offered to take Diego out for meals, or movies, or anything their heart desired, but they turned him down. Then he offered to help them prepare. They turned that down, too, only to find him helping Valentine instead.

The initial blush of fear Valentine had shown after learning of Maddox's past quickly vanished as the two men treated the Celestial Club's backstage area like their personal questing ground, their soft laughter echoing through the thin walls. Were he any other person who made Diego's heart thud like a war drum, they would have been overjoyed. What was theirs belonged equally to Valentine, always and forever. But the rate at which he was growing attached to Maddox scared them.

On the third night, they pulled him aside while Maddox worked on painting a forested wall panel for one of the upcoming events, noting with discomfort the adorable smudge of green that marked Valentine's cheek.

Diego squeezed his shoulder. "Please be careful."

"If it makes you uncomfortable—"

"No," they cut him off. "I mean, don't stop on my account. I'm just worried about you."

"I'm not handing out my heart. How could I, when it belongs to you?" The little cheeky tug of his grin made their own heart do things, soft and warm, entirely platonic but just as full and real as any romantic or sexual urge. His voice softened even further, his gaze darting back to Maddox. "But despite everything I know he's done, he feels *safe*. No one has ever felt safe to me that quickly… no one but you."

"Just be careful. We don't really know him yet," was all Diego could give in response.

They truly didn't know this new Maddox, but Diego

was quickly realizing that there was only so much of the man that they could handle before starting to drown in him—in his sincerity and passion and devotion—and they feared that if they did, their lungs would transform into things that survived purely on his oxygen, and they would never recover from losing him a second time. Despite Valentine's reassurances, they worried it was already going to happen to him. One of them, at least, had to stay whole enough to help the other move on.

So they restrained themself to short exchanges of out-of-character banter between event acts, trying to piece together who Maddox had become through superficial teasing and small talk.

"I can't believe you still have that bike. Isn't she ten years old now?" They asked, as though they couldn't mark on a calendar the exact date he'd received it, and every ride they'd taken between then and Diego's turning.

"Don't insult Juliet." Maddox lifted his knife threateningly, the juices of his dinner still clinging to the sides. "No one else would love her the way I do."

Diego batted the blade away. "You really can't let go, can you?"

They meant it to be a joke, but Maddox took the question seriously. "I can let go of a lot of things. Prejudice, vice, even my morals if that's what's needed to make the world better in the meantime. I can let go of anything that holds me back or brings more pain than good. But love? I'll always do whatever I can to keep that alive."

He stared so hard at them as he said it that it made Diego's heart flutter. They tried to let the feeling roll off them with a chuckle. "Then I wish Juliet a long and well-oiled life. Though if you replace enough of her parts, does she become the Motorcycle of Theseus?"

Maddox shrugged. "I think we've already established that people are allowed to grow and replace themselves and still be them, so why not personified vehicles?" The corner of his lips curled up. "But you can always touch *her* again too, if you'd like."

Diego might have stabbed him then for the blatant flirtation, if they'd thought they could get away with it.

Over the next few nights, they learned about more than just the ways his life had stayed the same, but also where it had changed, all their friendships in high school running dry, his relationship with his mother straining almost out of existence during his college years before his lack of income had left him crawling back to her.

"We're still not as close as we'd been, but she's slowly letting go of her vampire biases, so that helps."

"She's still living in that house by the lake?"

"Like she'd ever willingly leave that place. The area is getting more and more expensive though, and she's been struggling to keep up, especially with me leeching off her since my TV money dried up." He didn't sound remorseful about it. "But she signed a major deal with the Hughes doctors recently—you remember the Hughes, right? They just had their second kid. They named him Clementine, like the fruit. Can you imagine?"

"It's almost as bad as Maddox."

"Mh, yes, of course. *Clemmy* would be much better." His eyes sparkled as he said it.

Diego shoved him, gently. "You ever think about getting a job? Supporting *yourself?*"

"A paying job that's not acting? Please, that would ruin my flawless resume," he replied, though the snark seemed forced, like there was something deeper buried beneath. Something Diego did not want to dig up, lest it make them feel for him all the more.

It was better to keep Maddox at a distance. To keep their head above water.

Which would have been far more feasible, if only Diego wasn't expected to bite him in front of the entire court.

They refused him when he asked and stepped around the topic when their guests brought it up, laughing their denial off with a myriad of excuses, from a lack of hunger to a desire to test him further, and when the first two didn't suffice, to, "Princes are like fine wines; they taste better the longer you hold them in suspense."

The lack of blood was wearing on them, though. The Celestial Club provided its vampires with donated bags when they weren't working a role that partnered them with a human, but their stores were limited, so Diego was meant to be feeding off Maddox whenever possible for these three weeks. Every bagged sip they took to tide them over was one they were stealing from a vampire who needed it more.

But they could not, would not, sink their fangs into Maddox only to suffer for it later.

Their guests kept talking though, and worse, Valentine had begun pestering them during the live events too. He and Maddox would brush hands as they whispered, their gazes on Diego, so conspiratorial that it became part of their characters—the right hand of the vampire lord trying to make his sovereign jealous enough to finally succumb to their obvious yearning. By the fifth night of the event, it was growing harder for Diego to sustain the energy of their and Maddox's fictional relationship without some kind of new development.

It was the final night the club would be open for the week before their three-day break, and they had to give the crowd *something*. Not a bite. *Probably*, not a bite. But something...

Maddox sat at his customary seat during the premeal interactions, his attention for once not locked on Diego, but surveying the crowd with intense contemplation. He was just as beautiful caught up in something else as he was when his intensity was aimed at Diego. They lingered quietly behind him, letting themselves look at him for once. For the show of the thing. Their attention drifted naturally, from the corner of his jaw, down the lean length of his neck. When they weren't fighting to ignore it, the gentle pulse of his blood sang to them and his dry, oaky scent seemed to fill their lungs to bursting. They pressed a finger to their lips.

A taste might be safe enough, still. Just a quick prick, and then they'd withdraw.

Diego crept forward, so softly that when they ran a hand through Maddox's hair he startled. They tightened their grip, holding him in place. He went still. He didn't turn to look, just closed his eyes with a deep exhale, and let Diego tip his head to the side. In motions harsh enough to hide the shaking of their hands, they unclasped his half-cloak and pulled back his collar. Their nails dug into his skin—they could see the red marks they were forming as they grabbed the bared space of his shoulder—and still he didn't resist, didn't so much as make a sound.

He was laying himself out as a canvas for Diego, willingly trading his pain for their pleasure.

Right now they could press their mouth to his skin,

and he'd probably melt beneath it, or they could dig their fingers in until he bled, and he might let them lap at the wounds. If they bit him like this, he'd likely sigh at the first hint of venom—come from a few strokes of their hand beneath the table if they gave him enough of the blissful intoxicant. And Diego wanted that, wanted all of it. They could feel their apprehension and the pain of their past fighting the desire, but if they focused on craving, if they let nothing else in…

They bared their teeth and lowered their mouth to his neck. The moment their fangs touched his flesh, a wave of panic tore through them, not merely fear for the future, but horror in an exact replica of what they'd felt as he'd held the pliers toward them.

"Maybe if you pull them out."

They shoved Maddox away on impulse, catching themself just in time to play off the action with a bitter smile, like they had merely meant to taunt Maddox the whole time. A few of the guests laughed, but others called out in Maddox's defense. "Give it to him, he's earned it!"

Diego gave a disdainful huff and straightened their suit, swallowing down their rush of anxiety. This Maddy, whoever he was, had no pliers, no threats. They couldn't bite him, though, that much was obvious. Maybe they could stir up some other drama; Countess Amile's vampire had been just sassy enough tonight to warrant a challenge of her dedication. But as Diego stalked around the front of their small table, Maddox called from behind them.

"Am I not worthy yet?" He sounded just as fierce as always, but there was hurt there too. Playing to the sympathies of the crowd, damn him. He stood and stepped around their table, his fingers dragging along the shimmering cloth that covered it. "Because I will prove myself again, if I must."

Diego stilled. "Perhaps I merely find you... unappetizing." Everyone who had seen the way they'd looked at Maddox that first night—and every time his back was turned since then—knew that Diego craved him from his blood to his bones. This wasn't a truth; it was a challenge. *Can you make me cave,* Diego wanted to ask. *Make me forget myself, and then maybe I'll forget what you've done to me, too.*

One of his hands snaked out. He drew up his dinner knife with obvious contemplation. As he examined the blade, his other hand lifted to the side of his neck. He rubbed the skin there with two fingers, tilting his head like he was... finding the vein; threatening to spill his blood in such a quantity that Diego could no longer ignore it.

But splitting a vein in the neck with a blade was something only done with the utmost safety precautions, and never an act one was meant to do on *themself.* If he nicked a hair too deep, a vampire would have to be on him in seconds to start the healing, and even then there was only so fast that their venom and saliva could work. Yet as Maddox watched Diego, his fingers landed on the exact spot where Diego would have slipped in their fangs. A chill ran down their spine.

They scoffed, trying to unsettle both their own fear and Maddox in one go. "You wouldn't dare."

"For you, I'd dare anything." Maddox replied and lifted the knife.

Diego launched at him. They moved so fast that they had their hand around his before he even touched the blade to his skin. But as they went to yank it away, they felt his direction shifting. Despite his slower, weaker human body, he managed to twist Diego around, pulling their back to his chest like they were grinding slow dancers, his arms wrapped around them and his wrist conveniently in front of their mouth. With his scent so overwhelming, so *everywhere,* it was all they could do to keep themselves from pressing their nose to his skin and—

Fuck, this had been his plan all along, hadn't it?

Diego would have been impressed if they weren't so annoyed. They ducked free of Maddox's grip, and turned toward him as they elbowed him in the ribs. He took the blow with grace. Knife still in hand, he caught Diego by the thighs and lifted them onto his hips like they weighed nothing. He was so solid between their legs, and the ache for him that formed in their center was like a wildfire that rivaled even their craving for his blood. But they barely had time to think of that.

Maddox held the back of their head, guiding them toward his exposed neck. Venom pooled at the tips of Diego's fangs. Their body instinctively obeyed, senses honed to every shudder of his muscles, every pulse of his veins. Their nose brushed his skin first, burying in the hair that curled beneath his ear. Their lips touched, and finally a fang.

Then all they could see were his younger hands, knuckles white around those damned pliers.

Diego's whole body tensed. They jerked to the ground. Their heel caught the back of Maddox's knee, and he wobbled. They took full advantage, letting them both fall onto one side. Diego rolled them. As they came up on top, they twisted the knife from Maddox's grip and lodged a knee into his chest. They aimed the blade at his throat.

What Diego had done had barely been strenuous, but they were both heaving—exertion or emotion, Diego didn't know. Maddox stared up at Diego, and his lips quirked. A trail of blood dripped from a scratch on his neck. Where Diego's fang had cut, they realized.

Again, he hadn't been the one to flinch—Diego had. They were the one who couldn't handle this, not

Maddox. But as the murmurs of the crowd finally broke through their tunnel vision, they knew they could not let it look that way. As sovereign, they were the event's entertainment, and a weak, scared ruler who hid from the consort they were clearly attracted to would make for a terrible show.

Knife still in one hand, they leaned forward to draw its harsh metal along the cut, catching a droplet of red. They brought the blade to their lips and tapped their tongue to it, so lightly that they couldn't be sure what was taste and what was merely smell, before smearing the red between their fingers with a scoff. It took all of their strength not to shake apart or run or to collapse into Maddox's arms.

Instead, they sneered. "You dare too much, my dear consort. Try something like that again and I will strip you of more than those fancy garments."

They didn't help him up. But he seemed not to mind, following them back to their table with a look that bordered on adoration. As they sat, he drew the backs of his fingers against the side of their arm. "You're trembling."

"I'm fine."

"*Have* you been feeding?" He spoke low enough that the rest of the room couldn't hear—except perhaps Valentine, who didn't count—but Diego still worried they were coming too close to breaking character. And it was only the act that was keeping Diego together at the moment.

"Enough," they snapped. "Now sit, *consort*. Before I make you kneel."

Maddox huffed, but he sat obediently, his head bowed. He collected his dinner knife as soon as Diego set it on the table, before stealing their wine glass to down its contents. With the emptied cup in front of him, he began cuffing one sleeve. They didn't realize what he was doing until it was too late.

As calmly as if he'd done it a hundred times before, he slit open the vein in his wrist and angled it to drip in a slow but steady stream into Diego's cup.

They couldn't decide which they were more: impressed that he'd gone through with it, or pissed they hadn't been asked first. But maybe they weren't really that pissed at all, the fire in their chest a kind of thrilled anger, giddy and eager with just enough spite to make them mean. Because as sweet as the gesture was, they couldn't accept it. Diego might drink blood from a cup on the regular, but the lord of the vampires would never concede to that so easily.

Diego made a show of ignoring him, kicking back their chair and waving to Valentine. "You know, I think I'm hungry after all," they called, loud enough for the room to hear. "Bring me someone who's willing to do as they're told."

In response to the obvious slight, Maddox merely offered them a smile, and kept bleeding. He watched with an expression Diego couldn't quite read as the silver-haired gentleman from the first night of the event offered himself up, kneeling for Diego to casually peel back his sleeve. They pressed their lips to the man's wrist first, letting their gaze meet with Maddox's before sinking in their fangs. Maddox twitched—not a flinch, but a little jealous tightening. He lowered his eyes to the cup beneath his wrist, and still he kept bleeding.

Diego wondered, if perhaps they were being cruel to him.

It didn't matter, they decided as they let their prey return to his seat with a compliment and a kiss, their hunger sated without ever hitting the craving that coiled in their belly. Maddox wouldn't possibly bleed himself for their sake again. Especially not after Diego continued to ignore him, making him resolutely bandage up his wrist without the aid of a vampire's healing administrations, and asking Valentine to send the cup to Diego's favored vampire for the evening.

Maddox would get the message, surely.

When he left the moment the night ended, without a proper goodbye to anyone but Valentine, much less the offer of that date he'd been begging Diego for all week, they were certain he'd received *some* kind of message indeed. They feared he might have interpreted it as *fuck off, you'll never have me,* and worried, too, that it would be the right conclusion, even if the thought of losing his presence during events already made their chest ache. It left them such a distracted mess during their Wednesday night prep that they began running lines for the wrong event entirely before Valentine finally told them to take the practice off.

He'd sprinted after them as they stormed out, wrapping them up in the soft, timid embrace of his that always managed to make them feel like a complete person instead of a fragment of fire and wants. When he'd asked what was wrong though, Diego had just shrugged. They weren't ready to admit to anyone—especially their partner who was so clearly invested in Maddox—that they were terrified they'd accidentally driven him away. That they were still *enough* in love with him, that they genuinely wanted to know if they could fall in love with him *again*.

But when the doors opened again on Thursday night, and Maddox was the third guest to stride through them, somehow Diego's fears only shifted. Because if he was here, then he was still *theirs*, at least within the fiction. And Diego didn't know what to do with *that*, either.

Ten minutes before the meal was to be served, he sat down beside them, unwound the bandage at his wrist, and cut. He had learned nothing, clearly—and that—

that was his fault, wasn't it? It was his fault that Diego called forward another human from the guest list, granting them venom and a kiss in exchange for their blood as Maddox looked on, spilling his life source into a cup Diego couldn't accept. They gave it away again, and Maddox rebandaged his wrist without question.

He played out the rest of the night as though he'd done nothing out of the ordinary, though the other guests had clearly noticed. Gossip spread like wildfire. It varied in intensity, but always in Maddox's favor: he was valiant and Diego was torturing him. That belief didn't stop new humans from offering themselves up as substitutes though, nor Maddox from continuing to bleed for the one vampire he knew would refuse to drink of him.

It was too much—too much dedication and care and stupid, stubborn sacrifice. All for Diego. And each time that Maddox lost a little more blood, he asked for no vampire bite to aid in replacing it, nor saliva to help with healing. His own body was mending the recut flesh worse and worse. He tried to hide it from Diego, covering his winces and turning his increasingly more marred skin away from them, but they could see the way he was favoring it by the end of the weekend, how he'd stopped using his fingers whenever possible.

"You're going to hurt yourself," Diego finally hissed at him, as he held his bleeding wrist over their now nearly-full cup for the fourth night in a row. He tried to shift the wound so they couldn't see it as he pulled it back to bandage, but Diego grabbed his arm, scowling at the gnarly oozing line, the edges swollen and his skin red for an inch on either side.

"That's my choice." He tried to tug it free, but Diego refused to let him.

"Stop moving," they chided, a little too gentle for their character. If Prince Maddox had so wooed the court, though, then perhaps it was time for his charms to finally start rubbing off on their sovereign. "If it scars, it'll be harder to bite through later." They gave a little huff and snapped a finger over their shoulder. "Valentine, attend to this for me."

Maddox reached for Valentine's hand with his free one, wrapping up his fingers tenderly and squeezing, but he held them at a distance, his attention fixed on Diego. His expression was a destructive thing, his intensity so soft and melancholic. "Am I still not worthy of your care?"

Diego couldn't say no, not in the fiction they've been forging, and, they suspected, not in their real life either. Maddox had been kneeling at their feet for so long. Perhaps it was time to offer him a hand up. But—fuck, they didn't know if they *could* bite him. They could try, but how many times could they flinch away before he noticed—before everyone noticed? Maybe they could still give him something, though.

Valentine hesitated, but Diego offered him Maddox's cut wrist, like the limb was attached to a pet and not a person. "Venom only."

With the affection that had so quickly grown between Maddox and Valentine, Diego was not expecting the way Maddox deflated at the handoff, his gaze dropping to his lap. They instantly wanted his attention back, to see his eyes alight with joy and longing. With hope.

Valentine handled him gently, injecting venom into the vein above Maddox's weeping cut as he caressed Maddox's arm, and dramatically presented Diego the limb in return. They took it. They ran their thumb against the curves of Maddox's palm and tightened their grip on the dense muscles of his forearm. Just this touch, as platonic and practical as it was, made them yearn for more with a hollow aching, like they had a space within just waiting to be set on fire. Maybe they could not bring themself to bite him, but they could offer another gift, however small and insignificant.

The room had gone quiet, all eyes on the two of them.

With the pad of Maddox's bandage, Diego wiped away the oozing red. Then, they drew their tongue along Maddox's torn flesh. They could still taste the fresh seep of Maddox's blood, but it was light enough not to distract them—no more than the scent of him or the feel of his arm already did. His cut didn't close instantly into a new layer of seamless skin the way it would have had it been fresh, but with each tender drag of their tongue, Diego felt a little more of him knit back together. When the wound had closed enough to cease bleeding, they pressed their lips purposefully to the raised, reddened line.

It was no more than they'd done for any of the humans they'd drunk from that event, but with Maddox it left their head light and their heart in tangles. They let him go, not casting him aside for once but simply setting his arm onto the table between them. They traced the back of his hand as they pulled away.

He made a sound for them, soft and perfectly contented—or maybe he'd been making that sound all along. He'd gone loose in his chair, his whole body inclined toward them and his expression so satisfied that it made Diego's chest leap.

They took the cup Maddox had bled into and lifted it in a toast. "To commitment," They called, and the room echoed. They glanced toward Maddox with a smirk. "May your blood ever flow freely."

He bowed his head and clicked his wine glass to theirs.

Everyone sipped. The fullness of Maddox's blood hit Diego, sharp and deep and oaky like a dry Merlot, yet smooth as silk as it slid down their throat. They savored it, swallowing slowly, and wondered why they hadn't given in sooner. It wouldn't have fit the flow of the story, they reminded themself. Though looking out at the crowd, so many grins and sly glances their way, perhaps that was wrong.

"Thank you," Maddox whispered, smiling too. "That's not even Prince Maddox. Just Maddy."

"I know." It was growing easier and easier to tell the difference, to make out all the little complexities of him, even if Diego still felt like they didn't truly know this new him—the real him—beyond the strength of his dedication and the breath of his humor. "You are both delicious, by the way." Diego scowled. "But please don't bleed yourself for me again until I ask."

"*Will* you ask?"

They took another sip, and already the glass seemed too far empty. "Yes. And I think," they added, fangs bared, "that I'll be asking more of you very soon."

6

The rest of the night passed in such a blur that Diego didn't have time to fret over the after-hours challenge they were concocting for Maddox. Most of the guests had already departed by the time he emerged from the customer dressing space, his fantastical outfit traded for white-washed jeans with ripped knees and a leather riding jacket that had probably cost more than the motorcycle was now worth. He'd forgotten one strand of faux-gems in his dark hair, but somehow it only improved on the look. He was certainly beautiful enough to pull it off.

He lifted a hand to Diego, and for a moment it seemed like he was going to say something—ruin things, probably. But then he just gave a little bow and turned down the hall toward the side door.

Diego called after him. "Did you come here on Juliet?"

Maddox looked quizzical, but he answered a simple, "Yes."

"Bring her around."

"As you wish." The self-satisfied way he smiled while he said it made Diego want to shove him. Or kiss him.

"Inconceivable," they grumbled.

Maddox's voice shifted to a perfect rendition of Inigo Montoya. "I do not think that word means what you think it means."

Kiss or shove, they still couldn't decide. God, had his lips always looked this soft? Diego snorted. "Get the fuck out of my sight."

They walked away from him, hiding their grin.

Diego left a strand of their own gems in their hair. It wasn't on purpose, they told themself. It didn't *mean* anything. But they carefully tucked it in as they wrapped a bandana tightly over their long bob—yellow plaid to match the bright lines of their oversized flannel, which was baggy enough that they were able to trade their binder for a sports bra without an obvious difference.

When they emerged from the club, Maddox sat on Juliet, the bike running beneath him and the flap of his helmet up. He made as though to dismount.

Diego waved at him. "Scoot back."

His brow lifted, but he did as he was told. Diego slid onto the motorcycle. They'd ridden on and off enough since high school that the muscle memory returned in an instant, one hand testing the brake while the other gave the ignition a few revs. Maddox laughed and pressed his body against theirs. Their breath caught at the warmth of his chest, his large hands cupping their waist, long fingers firm but gentle as he fondled the curve where Diego's thigh met their pelvis. It sent shivers deep between their legs.

Diego smiled and let the bike fly. They shifted quickly through Juliet's gears, tearing down the empty early morning streets, basking in the rush of the wind and the freedom of the bike and the comfort of Maddox pressed so close, his life in their hands and their body in his. From the backstreets to the main streets, to the freeway and back again, they tore through the city until they were whizzing into a layer of sea-fog thick enough to turn the lights to distant stars in the gloom. They could smell the salt by the time they pulled onto an old dirt lot overlooking a grey expanse of nothing.

It was one of the few sequestered beaches left in a city that was quickly growing overridden, houses and shops pressed up to the sand and tourists thronging the waterline—not that even the most crowded tourist trap would have been particularly busy at this hour.

Diego shut off the bike, and together they dismounted. Maddox set his helmet on the handlebars and stared out into the gloom. The rush of the waves echoed through the mist.

He bumped his hip teasingly into Diego's side. His

whole being was so close, so in their space, that his warmth was like a fire against the chilly ocean breeze. "Ah, is your plan merely to get me to strip again, or are you going to go all the way this time and drown me for my impertinence?" As he asked it, he trailed his thumb down the side of their back and found their ass with a squeeze.

"Only if you keep *being* impertinent." Diego shoved him off, just hard enough to make him stumble. They set off purposefully toward the sand. "Walk with me."

Maddox laughed and caught up, scooping their hand into his, large fingers wrapped firmly around theirs. Diego grunted, but inside their heart fluttered. The sand shuffled beneath their boots, trying to pull them back down with every step, until they neared the water enough for the dampness to turn it into a compact layer. Diego still couldn't make out the waves despite their enhanced vampiric senses, and they wondered if Maddox's human vision was seeing anything at all.

He seemed not to mind, striding confidently through the darkness with his hand in Diego's.

"This is not what most people think of when they say a romantic walk on the beach," he teased.

"Since when have we been most people?" Diego shot back. They had adored that about their teenage relationship—still adored it in whatever this new spark between them was—but the words settled like a weight in their chest as they recalled the gnarled mess Maddox had made of his wrist just to prove his willingness to someone unwilling to budge for him in turn. Softer, they asked, "Have I been cruel to you, Maddy?"

"Perhaps. But I let you." He shrugged. "And I was a manipulative, stubborn ass. I just—I *never* want to stop fighting for you again. I don't fully know this new you yet, but the more I learn, the more I'm finding the thought of losing you absolutely unbearable. What has my life been without you, Diego?"

Diego snorted. "Healthy, probably."

"Healthy is for normal people." Maddox grabbed them by the shoulder, his grip shifting to the back of their neck as he pulled them towards him and he pressed their palm to his heart.

Diego shoved him away, a little harder this time, but that couldn't seem to wipe the smile from Maddox's face. Or their own. They shook their head and kept moving, fingers casually flexed for Maddox to take.

He reclaimed them eagerly.

As they walked, a cliff rose up on one side, rocks cutting shadowy figures in the fog. Through Diego's monochrome dark vision, the plants that draped down the sides looked grey and ominous. "I bet this place is beautiful during the day…"

"It's beautiful right now," Maddox replied, though Diego was fairly certain he could see nothing beyond the outline of their head and the scope of their shoulders. "We've always been creatures of the night."

"Yeah, but I still miss the sun. And the ability to go places that are only open during the day. To not have to plan every damn thing that isn't work around whether it'll fit into a human schedule and a human society, whether I can pass among them long enough not to get kicked out or called the cops on." They eyed him as they said it, trying to gauge how familiar he was with the actual life of a vampire. Finding pleasure from a pair of fangs was not the same as actually understanding the trials their bearer faced after the act was over.

Maddox nodded solemnly. "Sometimes a lord of the darkness just wants to stop by Blockbuster on their way home from work, but their way home from work is three-am."

"It's the little things," Diego agreed, pleasantly surprised.

"And the big ones." Maddox hesitated, before asking, "Has Serina replaced her window yet?"

"No. I don't think she'll dare until…" They almost said, *until the threat is dealt with*, but when would that be? Never, unless they did it themselves, and that was too dangerous a task to ask of the poor actors of the club. "One of our humans found a dead bat when she came to open this morning, but she couldn't tell if it was left there on purpose."

Maddox flinched.

They didn't blame him. "If we had someone who could intervene for us. Vampire police? Well, maybe not *police* exactly. After Rodney King..." They could still feel the bubble of righteous anger that had overtaken the city, turned violently inward when it became clear that no one who deserved it was going to suffer. A lot of other people had suffered instead, but Diego still wasn't sure that was any worse than if they'd let King's pain go like it was merely an ordinary consequence and not also a devastating travesty. Perhaps there were no good options when there were only bad people in control. "We need help, though. There has to be someone who can stand against anti-vamp organizations and won't immediately get murdered by them with no hope of justice, or else end up arrested themselves."

"Everything might still work out," Maddox replied softly, but his gaze dropped, and he seemed rather focused on the sound of the sand compressing under their weight. The shift made Diego curious; there was still so much about him that they didn't know. So much they still wanted to learn.

"What are you thinking?"

Maddox chuckled. "That I haven't been walking like this in ages. You know I never come to the beaches here? They just remind me of home, I think."

The sudden cheeriness to his tone surprised Diego

almost as much as the wistful melancholy. "I thought those were good memories for you?"

"Oh, they are. But they have you in them." He bounced his arm against theirs, as though to lighten the impact.

It lodged in Diego's chest all the same, thick and aching. He truly had centered his past around them, down to the very sentiments he felt for his birthplace. They understood; San Salud had stopped being home the moment the person they loved most there had betrayed them. Now that he was here again, the light seemed to return to those memories, bringing with it an unexpected ache for the place where their love had first blossomed. "Do you go back to San Salud much?"

"On and off," he added, "but it hasn't been the same."

"How's the city doing?" Diego forced themself not to sound like they missed it, then regretted the act as Maddox just shrugged, responding with equal casualness.

"Same as ever. Too many tourists in the summer, too many forgotten graves in the winter."

Even that was enough to bring visions of the crowded boardwalk, rollerbladers shouting and laughing in their bright pads and kids climbing on the rails, boats whizzing across the lake. The same tourists would flock to the city's numerous cemeteries in the evenings for gaudy ghost tours and historical recounting of the sanatoriums that had founded the city. There was one tour bus in particular that drove past Diego's childhood home at exactly 6:30pm every weekend evening from May to October.

It was an odd thing to fix emotion to, but there hadn't been much inside that house they cared for.

"Is my family... do you keep up with them at all? They uh, loved you." *More than me,* Diego didn't add. They had believed Maddox over their own flesh and blood, had threatened Diego in Maddox's defense while he'd been safe in his mother's house and Diego was panicked and hungry and in pain.

Maddox slowed, kicking at the growing number of pebbles in the sand. "They kept in touch for a few years."

"But?"

"They moved in '86. Didn't give out a forwarding address. No one even realized they'd sold the place until the U-Hauls drove out."

"They wanted to forget me." The laugh that lodged in Diego's throat was all bitterness. "Well, I guess that's not anything new."

"Diego..."

"No, I'm fine, really. I'd already figured I'd never see them again. Now we've both made it official." They still didn't want to linger on it though. There were better old memories; places and people they'd loved far more.

"Any other home news I should know about? Did the arcade close or the Fishnettery turn into a straight bar or something?"

Maddox, to his credit, obliged the topic change with grace. "The arcade is the same, though the Fishnettery's trying to expand. One of the wealthier men who frequented it died of AIDS last year, and he left them a plot of land right on the main street of the lakefront. The city doesn't want it there, but I think there's still hope it'll happen. Oh, Vitalis-Barron has started asking for vampires for their medical trials, and the vampire community is in a bit of an uproar over whether the pharmaceutical company is finally working on something that will help them or simply taking advantage of their desperation for anything that will pay people with fangs."

"San Salud has—" The word caught in their throat: vampires. Them. Like the Celestial Club, but larger than a single building, a single family. "A community?"

"In a sense. It's like the one here—a little disjointed, circles within circles. They're hard to find, let me tell you, but if you can break in once, it gets easier to hunt down others."

By the sounds of it, Maddox has accomplished that: the breaking, the hunting. Because he'd been guilty over what he'd done to Diego all those years ago? Or perhaps just for the thrill of it, the hope that he could find a vampire who'd sink their fangs into him the way he so desperately seemed to want from Diego. "Why look in the first place, if you're human?"

He merely shrugged. "Must my life be solely about me?"

The answer only made Diego's chest tighter. They bared their fangs. "You live in LA now, though? You've clearly found some of *our* vampires."

"I have an apartment here, and a house in San Salud—just a little one that I bought off the TV money."

A house, that he owned. "Wait, exactly how *much* TV money are we talking?"

Maddox lifted a brow. "You don't know? I thought for sure, with how you've been pushing me away…" He stared at them in disbelief a moment longer before shaking his head. "Well, fuck, I'm not bursting that bubble."

Diego slugged him in the shoulder with his own fist, still wrapped tightly around their hand. "Tell me!"

"No!" He laughed. "And don't you go looking it up, either. If you don't already know, then I don't want you to think of me that way. There's some parts of my work that are just things I'm doing—and I'm not ashamed of them—but I want you to know me like *this* first, no bells, no whistles, no offenses or awards, just me." Even in the darkness, the way he looked at Diego was a burning focus that made them feel undone in all the best and worst ways. Then his lips quirked. "When it was showing, I wondered a lot about your reaction to it, to seeing me. Who knew all that time I could have stopped fretting because *you* were living under a *rock*."

"It was a bridge, not a rock," Diego grumbled. "I was preoccupied with not being dead while spending way too much time wondering if maybe being dead was just the better option all around, then trying to recover from the hell of that while also helping the woman who rescued me. I only got back into living a few years ago."

"Ah." Maddox's intensity stayed on them, warm and full, even as his humor faded to a comforting solemnity, as though he were a wishing well, patiently awaiting their every secret. "I'm sorry. Your life has been brutal, and that was my fault."

He'd apologized so many times already, Diego didn't know why it was that one which broke them.

They forgave him. Whether they could make their stupid brain let go of the memory of his betrayal or not, *they* forgave him.

"It *was* your fault, but it was everyone else's too. You were easy to blame—you were the one who wielded the weapon that hurt me—but society constructed it and someone else would have brandished it if you hadn't. I'll keep hating that weapon with everything in me, but I refuse to keep hating you, Maddy. I fucking refuse."

They snatched his other hand, stole it like they were

proving a point taking possession of him, pulling him into their space with a growl. "And regardless of all that was done to me, and all the days I didn't want to keep living, I *did*, and I'm *happy* now—I will keep finding that happiness because that's a rebellion no one can take away from me. I love what I'm doing. It shouldn't be all I'm allowed to have in this life, but if it is, then it's going to be enough."

Maddox closed the little distance that remained between them, lacing their fingers together. He leaned down, his nose brushing their cheek, and Diego could feel his breath as he whispered, "It's not the *only* thing you have."

"Oh fuck off." They pushed him, closing in just as quickly as he stumbled away, not letting any space form between their bodies. Not wanting it to. "I thought this *wasn't* a romantic walk."

"Well fuck you too," Maddox growled. Then his lips were on theirs, fast and hungry, with all the power of a tornado, churning up Diego's fire into a breathtaking natural disaster.

They barely had time to think, to breathe, before his tongue was in their mouth, the taste of him filling them up. But Diego's body knew what they wanted, even if their mind was still struggling to catch up. They kissed Maddy back, fierce as the flame building through their core. Then they twisted their head a little too suddenly and their fang caught on Maddox's lip.

Diego's heart skipped. They jerked away. The panic didn't follow, nor the flood of memory, but when Maddox tried to grab them again, to force them back into the kiss, the club's safe word spilled out of them on instinct. "Nova."

Maddox let go. He stepped back, his hands locking behind his neck, and he looked about to drop to his knees on the wet sand. "God, sorry, I'm so sorry."

Diego punched his shoulder. That didn't release the bubble of pain and fear and bitterness that blistered through them unbidden, and they wrapped one arm around his waist instead, burying their face into his shoulder. Their lungs constricted. Their eyes burned. Slowly, they began to cry.

Maddox wrapped both arms around them. He held them closer and closer until his limbs felt like a shield, his heart a comforting hearth. Diego hadn't known they'd spent ten years in the cold until now, with his protective warmth on all sides. As their chaos of emotions passed, he fiddled with the tips of their hair where it stuck out from under their bandana. "It's my fault, isn't it?" he whispered. "The reason you won't bite me, it's because when you first told me your fangs had grown in, I asked you to… with the pliers."

"It was a long time ago. I look at you now, and I don't even see that person anymore. There's no reason—" Diego choked back an angry sob, ramming their forehead into Maddy's shoulder. "I should be stronger than this."

"I will start bleeding here and now if you talk like that." He pinned them to his chest aggressively enough to prove his point, but as he caught their chin in his large hands, he tipped their face towards his with the utmost tenderness. "You are *not* responsible for the way you internalize the trauma inflicted on you, only whether you turn around and inflict that pain on others."

"But I did—I hurt *you*."

"Yes, and as I said, I let you." He smirked, brushing his thumb along their jaw. "Also, I happened to like that pain. It turns out there's a reason I was so obsessed with every kind of bruise you could give me in high school."

Oh, fuck him. There had been a reason they worked so well together back then, and a reason they could still work, possibly better—and, Diego begrudgingly admitted to themself, healthier—than before, now that they both knew who they were and what they wanted. Diego couldn't predict where this relationship would take them both, especially when there was still a chance it could all crash and burn, but that was no reason not to enjoy the ride. Literally. "You said you have an apartment here somewhere?"

"Yes?" He looked suspicious in the very best way, breathless and a little desperate.

"I can't promise you my fangs, but how about you drive us there…" Diego bared their teeth, hooking two fingers into the edge of Maddox's jeans. "And we see what other ways I can hurt you."

7

Maddox's apartment was oddly unremarkable, just a regular old second story two-bedroom with a strip of balcony, the layout so similar to the one Diego shared with Valentine that they moved through it instinctively. Maddox had filled the space with secondhand furniture and landscape photography. The stack of VHS tapes beside his TV contained a variety of fantasy and romcoms, with an official copy of *The Princess Bride* below a recorded version with a homemade label. A stack of boxes in one corner still had *kitchen* and *bedroom* markered on them.

Diego waited for Maddox to close the curtains, trying not to let their earlier fears get the better of them. He knew exactly what he was getting into—had already candidly wooed Diego's partner for fuck's sake. They would take things one step at a time, and Diego would accept whatever came naturally, whether that was simply a fun night of sex or a full continuation of the romance they'd started as teenagers, with or without fangs.

The knowledge felt like a weight lifted off Diego's shoulders. As much as they loved the club, being the leader of a three-week long story came with a lot of expectations on what and how they were meant to give themself away. Here, in the privacy of Maddox's home, Diego could let themself explore with the same freedom and security that the club's guests paid for.

When Maddox asked, "What would you have of me, my lord?" Diego knew exactly what they wanted.

"Strip." They bared their fangs, running their tongue along the point of one. "I want you lightly flayed and served to me, preferably on a stake."

Maddox's gaze was life itself. "It would be my honor."

He started with his jacket, sliding it off his shoulders and tossing it dramatically over the back of the sofa. His fingers hooked in the collar of his t-shirt, then trailed down, tracing the defined lines of his chest through the fabric, before hooking into the top of his jeans instead. He grinned.

Under the modern, white-washed denim he had on a new pair of the same silken boxers he'd worn the first day he'd burst into Diego's work, and it delighted them that they were his typical style. Diego was too ravenous just to watch any longer, grabbing the edges of his pants and shoving them down. As he stepped out of them, laughing, Diego made quick work of their own jeans, then wiggled their sports bra out from under their flannel, tossing it to the side. Last, they untied the bandana from their hair.

Their string of the Celestial Club's fake sapphires and diamonds still hung safely in place. It felt right to have them there, a piece of their new home staying with them even as they gave a part themself back to their old one.

Maddox's shirt joined their pile on the floor, leaving him, once more, in nothing but his silken underwear and that single strand of gems to match Diego's. This time though, Diego was not circling at a distance. They pressed their hands to his abs, running them up and across in rough, hungry motions, trying to touch every bit of him that they'd lost over the last ten years. Somehow Maddy belonged to them again, impossibly and perfectly, and they were going to make their mark on him, brand him so deep he never strayed again; this beautiful, stubborn man who pushed and fought like he had already decided he would die at their feet, but froze, too, at a single safe word.

As his fingers found the top button of Diego's flannel, they felt no hesitation in saying, "I'd like to keep the shirt on."

Maddox hummed thoughtfully, leaving the buttons alone. "I remember you never liked to be touched there."

"So you knew that part of me even before I knew myself?" Diego could not have anticipated how happy that would make them, nor how seen.

"Your chest was so beautiful, I didn't understand why you were never into it. But it makes sense now."

"And you don't mind?" Diego refused to care whether anyone—Maddox included—would be disappointed in how they chose to live within their own body, but it made them sad to think that Maddox might have to miss a piece of the old them he'd once enjoyed.

The heat in his gaze set fire to their soul though, as he surveyed down the sweep of their neck and the lines of their arms, across their pelvis and between their legs, to where Diego could feel a very particular warmth growing, their body begging to be touched by more than merely his gaze. "All of you is beautiful," he said. "I have plenty else to focus on."

Diego had never felt more like a *he*—more like *himself*—in all his time as a lover. Magnificently, they felt no less genderless for it either. With Maddox, Diego could contain multitudes: they, and he, and starlight and fire. There was no part of them—of him—that his Maddy would touch that didn't feel like home.

They grabbed Maddox by the neck and kissed him, rough and zealous. Maddy returned it with just as much passion. His face tipped to the side and he grabbed with his teeth, tugging: possessing. His scent flooded Diego's senses. They could taste the first hints of him, like a craving at the back of their tongue.

All thoughts of an orchestrated, deliberate scene derailed from Diego's mind. Maddox was already leaning down, but they lifted onto their tiptoes to deepen the kiss, gripping onto his shoulder and into his hair, letting their nails bite his skin until Maddy hissed with pleasure. He grabbed them by the ass, lifting them up to balance them on his waist. They kissed down on him, wrapping their legs tight around his back, and, riding on nothing but the sensation of the moment and the presence of the man beneath them, they grabbed his lower lip between their teeth and bit.

Their fangs pushed into tender flesh, fast and hard and without so much as a hint of the venom that was building within: all pain, no pleasure. The way Maddox gasped was a kind of decadence all of its own. His knees wobbled. One hand left their ass as he caught himself on the armrest of the sofa.

Diego took their time to suck the wound closed, drawing out as much of Maddy's blood as they could in the process. He nearly lost his grip on them again by the end, moaning into their mouth. Even without their venom, he was breathless and undone, and his hands on Diego held a frantic possessiveness, like he wanted all of them, all at once. He braced on the sofa armrest, dragging his fingers against the soft fabric of Diego's underwear in a motion that sent shudders through them.

"Where—what—do you want?" he asked.

Diego smirked against his mouth. "Take your chances."

He pressed his fingers harder, unfolding Diego beneath the fabric until he found their sweet spot. Diego groaned and shifted against the touch. The ache deep inside them turned to a blaze, white hot where he'd began to rub, so fast and desperate that it sent Diego curling against him. They grabbed the lobe of his ear with their teeth, and he moved even quicker against the slickening garment, matching their aggression with wild passion. As Diego came against his touch, they sank their fangs into his neck, venomless and forceful, consuming him. He cried out, and their whole body felt aflame.

Maddox shoved his fingers under the side of the fabric and pressed them into Diego's rhythmic tightening, dragging in and out. Diego rode from their peak into something vaster and steadier and just as lovely, gradually climbing once more with each press of Maddox's hand into them. He trembled beneath them, his head back and his eyes half closed.

Diego breathed against his neck, lips still slick with his blood. "Do you still want my fangs?"

"I want them," he whispered.

"Then beg."

Maddox wasted not a moment, his speech like a prayer in time to the fingers he still thrust in and out of Diego. "Bless me with your bite; tear me asunder. My god, I want you to make me bleed for you. Make me bleed until you're satisfied or there's nothing left of me."

Diego hooked one leg onto the sofa's armrest and shoved Maddy onto the cushions. They bit down again. His fingers slid out of them, snagging on their underwear, but as he pulled free, Diego tore the fabric off entirely, relishing the way they dripped along their own thighs as they scooted back between Maddy's legs and lowered their fangs once more to his flesh. They fed from the tender skin of his inner thigh in rushed, venomless bites they barely took the time to close. Maddox writhed and cried out, whispers of *please* between his hushed screams. As Diego neared the fabric of his boxers, his hard length still straining beneath, he nearly kicked them from the intensity of his jerking.

They pinned his legs beneath their own and grabbed at his underwear. He went so still that Diego froze as well, watching him with their fangs bared. The way he lay there, half propped up by pillows, his curls mussed and his cheeks red, his skin littered in the bright red of half-healed bites—he was incredible—but it was his expression that intoxicated Diego, the way he could be this obedient yet look at them like his submission was the very furthest thing from docile, made of fire and wind and lightning.

"You're the most handsome being I've ever seen," he whispered.

Diego smirked. "Compliments won't save you now, Maddox Burke."

"I'm degraded to a full name?" He laughed, the sound husky and shallow. "And here I thought I was yours."

As he spoke, Diego pulled open his boxers. The space between their thighs shivered at the sight of him. They gave him one languid stroke, up and back down, tightening their grip at the end. "Oh no, you're absolutely mine. Every little bit of you." They licked their fangs and ran a nail over the glistening end of his erection with a precision that made him jerk and whisper. Their grin widened. "I think I know where all your blood is going."

Leaning in, they dragged one of their perfectly pointed canines along his swollen length, tongue following behind. They could feel the reservoir of their venom fighting to break free just beyond the tip of each fang—it was taking all their willpower to hold it back—but hold it back they did, making Maddox sob gently under his breath. He had plenty of time to offer them a safe word, one to pause or to slow or to turn back entirely, but the syllables that left his lips were all those in Diego's name.

So they bit him again.

This time when their fangs sank through his flesh, driving deep into the sensitive skin of his dick, he made a noise like a creature possessed, a fucked-up sound that was as satisfying as it was delicious. As it faded, Diego let loose all the venom they'd been storing until then. Maddox's vocals changed to ones of shocked delight. He arched, his toes curling and his fingers clutching at Diego blindly.

"Oh—fuck," he managed.

Diego withdrew their fangs, his blood still oozing from the pin-pricks. They were suddenly aware of just how much further they were pushing Maddy than anyone they'd ever laid their fangs on before, and a flicker of panic ran through them. "Are you okay?"

"Yes!" He gasped the word, squirming again as another wave of tension seemed to roll through him. "It's like I'm coming, but it keeps—it just keeps—" His fingers found their hips, and he cried, "Turn around."

A flush ran through Diego. They swept a finger along the blood still trailing down Maddox's length. "Who's giving the orders here?"

"Turn around, *please*." He sat up a little further, but he seemed to need to cling to Diego to do it. "Let me— let me bleed inside you."

Between the taste of him already saturating their senses and the grip of his hands on their skin and the heat that was still ripe and heavy between their legs, the mere thought of Maddox within them, the little cuts their fangs had made rubbing with each thrust, set them on fire. They turned, making every shift an act of ownership as they positioned him against the slickness of their front opening. He held them from behind, continuing to shudder and gasp like he was riding crest after crest, but as Diego sank down onto him, both their pleasures seemed to crash together into a firestorm.

Diego groaned, riding Maddy harder and faster with each plunge. They grabbed his arm—their nails slid into the still only half-healed line of reddened flesh he'd been cutting open for them each night. Bringing it to their mouth, they sank in their fangs, not bothering to hold back their venom this time as they drank in ragged gulps to match the slide and drop of their fucking. The flavor of him had turned, like the pressure inside them, to something that wasn't a sense or a sensation at all, but starlight and pure ecstasy.

Maddox sobbed, biting into the flannel on Diego's shoulder like it was all he could do to anchor himself. His free hand gripped at their waist, then past, shoving between their legs to rub desperately at the most swollen, sensitive part of them. They bucked instinctively against the force of his touch, biting down harder, but he held them in place, refusing to let up as they peaked into a long sparkling haze, and again in a blistering rush of white. As they tightened around Maddox the second time, he groaned and stiffened once more, stilling his fingers as he came into them. Diego relaxed to the comfortable spread of his warmth, grateful that the club had an improvised stash of morning after medication on hand just for times like this.

As their high faded to a steady contentment, they licked Maddox's wrist wound closed and drew themself off him. His blood was smeared into the slickness they'd left on him, and they closed those final little bleeding marks with a gentle kiss. "You were glorious."

"Does this mean I've officially earned your acceptance, my lord?" Maddox teased, limp against the couch and a smile on his lips.

"Fuck off," Diego gave him a mock shove in the ribs, but they returned his smile without hesitation. "Except don't, because you're not allowed to leave me ever again."

"I hadn't planned to." He didn't look away, didn't even blink, his focus on them so hot and bright he could have been their sun—the one they'd enjoyed as a human. He made the night beautiful. His expression wrinkled as he tried to shift positions and winced instead. "I might want to shower though, and then sleep until noon. Are you going to join me for that?"

"I suppose I have to see you cared for, don't I? Since you *are* mine." They leaned over him and pressed their lips to his, fangs and all. "My Maddy."

♛

Maddox looked so small while he slept. Diego had forgotten that: the way he'd bow inward, burying his face into his pillow. Every now and then he'd make a little noise, delicate and mysterious, neither happy nor sad. Diego ran a hand through his hair, waiting for his tension to ease once more, before slipping quietly out of bed.

His computer dialed up with such a loud series of noises that their heart jumped into their throat. Maddox only curled tighter with another tiny sound. Diego tried to relax. Maddox only curled tighter with another tiny sound. Diego tried to relax.

They told themselves this wasn't a transgression—it was their right to know. If Maddy had been awake, he'd only have argued for a minute before giving in and showing it to them himself. Still, they felt a little cruel as they clicked open the internet browser and clumsily navigated to the search engine. They'd only been online a few times since the worldwide web had sprung into more prominent use over the last year, but they figured there had to be some record of—

There: a movie and television show database.

Diego typed in Maddox's name.

Maddox Burke, lead actor in Red as Blood (1988-1990), where he played the role of Brennen McGale, a famous vampire hunter who...

Diego's blood pounded in their ears. *Vampire hunter.* Fuck, he'd played a hunter—and not just any hunter, but the glorified kind that always appeared in these popular dramas, where vampires were fetishized monsters who lived only to be fucked or killed, usually one then the other. He'd let himself become the face of that awful stereotyping, the valiant vampire murderer that so many humans clung to the idea of. The hero they emulated when they threw bricks through windows and left dead bats outside doorsteps.

Diego forced themself to breathe, to focus. This was exactly why he hadn't wanted them to know; he hadn't wanted the knowledge of what he'd done to cloud the fact that he'd *changed*. He wasn't the selfish teenager who'd come at Diego with a pair of pliers, and he wasn't this malicious actor either. While he'd hidden this from Diego, he'd been very clear that he had quit television because what he was doing hadn't sat right with him.

That was Maddox's truth. It had to be.

Still, Diego's heart beat in their ears as they finished

the summary.

...a famous vampire hunter who struggles with his lust for an immortal vampire seductress through all three seasons, eventually killing her to save his high school sweetheart and fellow vampire hunter.

They shut the browser down.

Their hands shook, but they flexed and tightened them, reminding themself of how Maddox had felt beneath their fingers. How he'd begged for their bite. But that only made them wonder if his hunter character had begged the terribly-portrayed mythical vampire on his show for the same thing. What they had was not an act; the way Maddox looked at Diego—that couldn't be fake. Why would he feign that?

Diego turned the computer off, but they couldn't make themself climb back into bed, to lay beside his sleeping presence, so tight and restless, and envisioning his face on *Red as Blood* poster. A few minutes—they just needed a few minutes to themself. To process.

The room swam around them, and when they opened the bathroom, they found rows of hanging shirts. Wrong door. They nearly closed it again, but their gaze caught on the massive lock box on the floor, a heavy-duty case made to be carried by someone with Maddox's height and strength. They should have let it go. They would have, probably, if their brain wasn't whispering doubts, their fangs aching at the base like someone had wrapped a pair of pliers around them and pulled.

Surely it wouldn't open for them.

But when they entered Maddox's old pin combination the lock popped free.

Diego knew what was inside the moment they lifted the lid, a burning heat radiating along their skin and tearing at their strength. Still, they forced themself to look long enough to lodge the sight of it into their memory. Knives, zip ties, a gun, and the source of their pain: a series of holy silver chains, ranging in size and weight but all of them bursting with power. These were not stage props, not even amateur anti-vampire paraphernalia—this was genuine hunter gear.

Diego snapped the case close. They had been apprehensive before, but now they were truly scared, their head light and their nerves on fire. Their legs wobbled as they stood and they had to grab at the closet door for support.

This was still just Maddox though—Maddox who'd been visiting the Celestial Club for most of the month, who'd bled for Diego and begged for their bite. Who'd played a television hunter for three years. And who had a lock box of authentic hunter gear.

Diego didn't want to believe it.

But if those items *were* his....

Why own weapons made specifically to harm

vampires if he didn't mean to use them? Perhaps he could have been given them by someone, someone who hated vampires enough to want them dead and who'd thought Maddox was the kind of person who agreed? But then he'd chosen to *keep* them. The only reason to hold onto holy silver—to not find someone who could unmake it, remove its deadly effects on vampires and turn it back into its composite metals—was with the intention to use it someday. He might have decided that, for the moment, Diego and Valentine were worth more to him as potential partners than as victims, but how long would that last? If he could change once—if he ever really had changed in the first place—then he could change again.

He could go back to being the same selfish teen who'd ruined Diego's life the instant his love and lust for them ran out. And this time he wouldn't be holding pliers, but weapons made to trap and burn and kill. This time, the vampire he wielded them against would end up dead.

They closed the door, slumping down its side as their knees gave out. Their gaze locked on Maddox's sleeping form, every rise and fall of his shoulders urging them to run. He had looked so vulnerable to them just minutes ago. So small and fretful. Not a predator, but a prey-thing, one they'd been proud to claim, heart, mind, and body.

Maybe there was something Diego had missed. *Maybe*—they hoped.

They could always ask him. A spark of fear rushed through them at the thought. If their doubts were true, there was no telling what he'd do when confronted. And if he hadn't been sincere all this time, how would they know if he wasn't still lying to them?

It was terrible, and it was foolish, and it was probably a trap made of their own mind and their turbulent emotions. Maddox loved them. Maddox was theirs. But if he wasn't… if he was a hunter, and Diego was a vampire…

Then they would not be the first vampire to die because a hunter had taken them to bed.

Diego counted their own breaths, staring above Maddox at the crack in the curtained windows where the sky was just beginning to lighten. If they stayed past dawn, they wouldn't be able to leave without their skin fully covered and a ride to whisk them home. They would be trapped in this apartment with their doubts festering in their mind, waiting for Maddox to wake at any moment. They needed space; space to think this through, sort out the truth from the lies, calm the trembles in their spine and warm the chill from their skin.

And they needed Valentine.

Whatever happened, Maddox was not their only

soulmate, merely the one who could sob their name like a prayer while they fucked him; the one they'd recarved space for, in their heart, in their lungs, even knowing how badly he'd once hurt them. If it turned out they'd been right when they'd denied him in the beginning, they didn't know how they'd live with themself.

8

Interlude

Maddox had dreamed of Diego, of their sharp smile and the brilliant weight of them. Not them—*him*.

"*They for my friends, he for my lovers.*"

And *he* was Maddy's lover.

He was, Maddox tried to convince himself as he drew the note off the counter: *Had to go rescue Valentine. Thanks for the blood. Xoxo D.*

It didn't break his heart, exactly—a part of him had been waiting for this. He'd pushed and he'd pushed, and Diego had given in. And now they were retracting. Reclaiming the power. Putting back up their walls.

He'd hoped, stupidly, that maybe their relationship had grown past those kinds of vicious cycles they'd ravaged each other with in their youth, but it seemed they'd only transformed into something new; distance in place of barbs. Well, this version cut into him just the same. Perhaps worse. He thought he preferred Diego's confrontational battery to this coldness. At least then, they'd been with him.

He crumpled their note, dropping it in the trash on his way to the closet. The box was just as he'd left it, safe and locked. Maddox selected his weapons with more care than usual, his mind running recklessly to Diego's skin beneath each, all the myriad of ways that harm could be inflicted on even the strongest of vampires. He held that thought as he slipped the deadly gear into place.

Whatever Diego did, he could not forget why he had come. Or who he was fighting for.

9

"You have to talk to him." Valentine stood in their apartment's tiny kitchen, both hands around his coffee mug and his fangs halfway retracted. His pinky bounced anxiously against the purple ceramic, revealing the text *My New Name is Daddy* in jerky flashes.

Diego leaned both elbows against the counter, trying to ignore the knot in their gut. Bile clung like a stain in the back of their throat where Maddy's blood had so gloriously lingered twelve hours earlier, and their body seemed like it couldn't decide whether to be afraid of him, angry at him, or angry at themself instead. "But what if I'm right?" they hissed. "He had *holy silver* in his closet. I'd finally stopped seeing his grip on those damn pliers every time I tried to bite him and now this? I don't know how I'm supposed to feel, or think, or—" They groaned, dropping their head into their hands. "I hope he's the person I've been falling in love with again—I hope he's really changed—but I can't know for certain."

"He's been dedicated to you since he showed up.

And not only you, Diego. He's so sweet to me, and he doesn't care that I'm not interested in the traditional trappings of romance or sex. He's attentive and thoughtful, like he wants to be *ours* and not just yours. That means more than I can express… more than I ever thought I'd have from someone who clearly wants so badly to fuck you." His gaze lowered to his mug. "Maybe I'm biased, but you're brighter with him around, brighter and fiercer and more alive, and I don't want you to lose that over something that could all be a misunderstanding."

Diego cringed, because it was true. "It's not that *you* don't make me feel alive. Because you do; you know that, right?"

"I know, Eggy." Valentine smiled, not a hint of jealousy in his expression, only love and hope. "But I also know we don't share all the same things you do with Maddox, and while that doesn't bother me, it's something you crave out of life, and you deserve a relationship that can give you that. Not *instead* of me, obviously, just like, *in addition*." A touch of pink rose in his pale cheeks. "Besides, I kind of like the taste of his blood? Not in the sense you do, I'm sure, but it's soothing in a way a lot of blood hasn't been for me. I want to believe that he wouldn't feel this much like home if he was secretly planning to murder us."

"Sentimental Lentil," Diego grumbled and wrapped

their arms around him. Valentine leaned against them, and they could feel the tension slowly ease from his body. "What if he *is* everything he presents himself as, and my doubts push him away?"

"If he's that man, then he won't balk because you confront him," Valentine reminded them, sounding far too reasonable about something that felt so much to Diego like the end of the world. He hummed softly. "Have you told Serina yet?"

"No."

His brow lifted.

Diego grunted and shoved him in the shoulder, receiving a snort, then a curse as his coffee spilled. It made the world feel a little less terrible. "I feel like I need more information before I go to her with it. She really wanted to believe in Maddox, but she has so much on her plate with the Paladins' threats, and if it turns out Maddox is one of them..." Diego shook their head. "I'll tell her, but I want to know enough that I can actually bring her something useful first."

"Just don't wait too long, okay?" Valentine kissed Diego's cheek, and they let him hold them, and wished that every relationship could be this easy.

If this was anything else, it would be so simple. If Diego wasn't a vampire, and Maddy didn't have the tools that killed their kind stashed in his lock box. They almost wished they could just unsee it all, that they could have left well enough alone. But that wouldn't have actually solved the problem. Not that they were solving the problem like *this* either.

They spent their days off at the club, avoiding Valentine's questioning looks and ignoring Maddox's calls. They left him quick messages on his answering machine in the middle of the night—they were busy, they'd had chores they'd been ignoring, the club needed an extra pair of hands, whatever excuse they could come up with. All through Wednesday practice, their brain was in shambles once again.

As much as they hated it, they just had to ask him. They could meet in a safe place—hunting was technically not legal, in the strictest of terms, so a well-lit, populated area might deter him from making any moves. And if Maddox wasn't the man he'd made himself out to be, finding out now, under their own terms, would give them as much power as they were likely to get in this situation. After the meeting, they'd at least have something more to bring to Serina. It had to happen in the next eighteen hours though, before the doors opened for the week's first event session and Maddox showed up in his regal costume, dashing and chivalrous and offering to bleed himself out at Diego's feet.

When they called to ask him out for coffee before the club, though, he clammed up.

"I have something I can't miss then."

"Work?"

"Yes—no. It's complicated." He sighed, such a deep, uncomfortable sound that Diego could picture him rubbing his neck. The image made their fangs fill with venom. Their stomach flipped as they realized just how instinctual the idea of biting Maddox had already become. "I'll tell you about it later," he added. In their teenage years, that would have meant he was genuinely planning to explain the thing, accurately and in detail, letting Diego ask questions and sling accusations and sometimes fists. But Diego didn't know if that held true, anymore.

It turned out, they didn't know him after all.

They hummed noncommittally, replying with a grumbled, "Well fuck you, too" that they hoped they'd successfully played off as teasing, and ended the conversation.

Something he couldn't miss, something that was work but wasn't... it was all too coincidental. Maybe *this* was the proof Diego needed. They wouldn't have to ask him, wouldn't have to put themself in that kind of physical danger. Then, if he did come to tell them himself afterward, they'd know the facts ahead of time, could gauge his honesty and prod at his secrets. These were all technically excuses, Diego knew—it was the emotional danger they were afraid of. But it turned out that was scarier than any other dive into the unknown.

Diego wrapped themselves in the thickest fabrics they owned, threw on their biggest pair of sunglasses beneath their tinted helmet, and borrowed the old motorcycle one of the club's other vampires occasionally lent out. They parked in the shadow of the building across from Maddy's, hanging out behind the dumpsters in case he was watching for anything suspicious. He couldn't know that they were onto him. Probably. Maybe.

It was better to be safe than sorry.

Despite all their layers, by the time Maddox pulled away on Juliet, Diego was already suffering from the first hints of sun-poisoning. They tried to ignore the ache setting into their bones and the shivers that started in their limbs—this was still their best option; information without confrontation—and pulled out far enough behind him not to be obvious. They kept their distance, hanging to the sides of the street where the least of the late afternoon light could reach them, as Maddox made his way towards… the Celestial Club?

He turned the wrong direction when he reached their street, though, heading five blocks down and three past before veering into an alley. Diego slowed enough to listen for the telltale cut of Juliet's ignition. They hid their own bike in an alley and snuck around the corner in time to watch Maddox enter a run-down two-story warehouse.

Diego's stomach twisted. This proved nothing—there had to be a dozen reasons he could be hanging out at a place like this that had nothing to do with hunters or vampires. They just couldn't come up with any of them in the moment, because their heart was pounding too violently to think straight.

They slipped off their helmet, keeping to the shade as they jogged quietly down the alley. At the first possible window, they peeked inside. Through the grime on the glass, they could make out battered cement floors and plastic folding tables, twenty or so people gathered around with weapons. They weren't all as fancy or large as the ones in Maddox's closet, but Diego recognized the gleam of their holy silver. The group waved to Maddox as he entered. Like he was their friend.

Like he was one of them.

Because he was—Diego could see it as they watched, frozen in place as though the sight had put a spotlight on them, and yet they still didn't want to believe it. They had come because they thought they'd be proven wrong, they realized. Because the Maddy who'd bled for them, laughed with them, moaned beneath them, couldn't possibly be doing *this*. But here he was, slapping a man on the shoulder as he showed off the holy silver chain he'd looped around his wrist.

Diego stepped back. Their legs felt numb, the

ground a wavering cloud. It was true. Maddox was—he was—

"Well, what do we have here?" A man sneered behind them in a tone he probably thought was flirtatious but would have lit up every bone in Diego's body even if they hadn't been a vampire lurking outside a meeting place meant for hunters.

They checked that their fangs were fully retracted and turned. As they did, the man shifted his grip on something silver. A soft burning sizzled along Diego's exposed skin, sinking deep into their muscles and zapping their strength. They hissed instinctively, baring their teeth. All their teeth.

He hadn't expected a vampire, Diego realized, just a person—a woman, probably—pretty enough to warrant his harassment and alone enough to have to bear it. But the realization sank in and his expression turned from sexist leering to something even more hideous. He held his holy silver cross out in front of him like a priest in a movie, his hand on his belt where Diego could see the hilt of a knife prodding up from under his jacket. He whistled—not a catcall but a summons. "You got some holy silver in there you can spare? Because we're going to need it."

Every cell of Diego's body told them to run, straight back the way they'd come, hoping their weak, shaking legs would carry them past the man in time to burst across the street. But they knew what happened to vampires caught in direct sunlight when holy silver was near, had heard enough stories of the way their skin would crackle and their bodies turn to ash. That was the one thing the media always seemed to get right—the one way a vampire could die that was fully unique to them.

The other end of the alley then; maybe if they circled back around…

But as Diego stumbled away from the hunter, two more burst out from the old warehouse, more holy silver in their hands. Diego tried to scoot around the new arrivals, but their feet were more unsteady with each step, their lungs growing increasingly tighter. They could feel the phantom grip of Maddox's pliers around their fangs—a memory from a timeline that hadn't even happened, the fear of it lingering so long and strong that it might as well have. It wouldn't end there, though.

A vampire was still a monster, even without their fangs.

And whatever the Celestial Club liked to pretend, in the real world, monsters weren't loved, they were slain.

Diego hurled away from the hunters as fast as they could under the holy silver's influence, but one of the men grabbed them around the waist and the other latched onto their arm. They shifted their momentum to lunge for the nearest throat, but a chain of silver tightened around their neck, heavy and solid and identical to Maddox's. Even with their thick scarf still separating their skin from the metal, it sent a terrible ache through their chest and scorched at the underside of their chin. The hunter yanked backward on the chain. Diego crumpled.

They bit back a sob, struggling at the holy silver with their gloved hands. Everything felt a hundred pounds too heavy, every sensation buried beneath the throb of the metal. Two of the hunters grabbed Diego under the arms and dragged. The world blurred and darkened, churning into light and shadow as they were pulled into the building, until all they could make out was Maddox turning towards them.

He was beautiful. Even now, like this, so terrible and awful, with his expression lofty and a knife bobbing in his hand, his intensity and passion and poise as manifest as ever. He was beautiful; and he would kill them.

The first hunter who'd come upon Diego in the alley shoved at their back, only to yank the chain around their neck tighter as they fell to their knees. "Look what we caught snooping around outside."

Diego choked against the holy silver. Their head felt light. Maybe no one would get to kill them. Maybe they would just die like this, on their own, under Maddox's piercing gaze.

He snorted, tossing his knife once and slipping it back into his belt. "What you caught," he said as he stepped toward them, "is a tamed bat. *My* tamed bat, to be precise."

His... what...?

Diego's mind felt like it had come to a stuttering halt, but as he wrapped his hand around their jaw, looking into their face, they could think of nothing but him: of his eyes on them, sharp enough to cut. "You little *starlit* bitch, I thought I told you to stay with the bike. You know naughty bats get barbecued."

*Star*lit. Star*light*. The emphasis caught Diego in the chest. One of the Celestial Club's safe words—but not just any safe word; it was a prompt. Both a clarification that they were happy to proceed and a question as to whether the other person would be comfortable moving forward with them. A request for permission.

Why the hell would he be asking *their* permission, unless...

It was an act.

He could have been playing with Diego. He would know this word might be soothing enough to convince them to drop their guard. But Maddox *already* had all the power; he could have had their throat slit, had them bound and laid at his feet, taken whatever he wanted without ever uttering that offer of safety. And he'd claimed them. He had to be acting—so convincingly that Diego almost believed he truly thought they were his tamed vampire. He'd been the one to beg for them and bleed for them, and he was quoting their own safe word to them now. What option did they have but to trust him?

Maddox had a lot to answer for, but at least wanting Diego dead wasn't part of it. They just had to survive long enough to demand the full truth. And, perhaps, to apologize for doubting him.

"I…" Fuck, playing the submissive side was harder than they remembered from the few awkward times they'd tried it at the club.

They focused on Maddox's hands, those hands he'd used to cut himself open for them night after night. This was between the two of them; the two of them alone. A gift, in exchange for what he'd already given them.

"I couldn't bear it, master." They let their shoulders shake with every ounce of emotion and sun-poisoning already wrecking their body, and pleaded, "I just wanted to see you."

Maddy—their Maddy, whose game they still weren't sure of, but who they were throwing all their trust into— let his fingers dance over the holy silver around their neck. "How precious," he hummed. Then he shrugged to the hunters gathered around. "I doubt they'll be needing these. They'll be a good little bat." Like he couldn't have cared less, he tugged the chain looser and pulled it over their head.

It scorched for a moment as it passed over the bare

skin of Diego's face, but the heat of Maddy's gaze kept them in place. They buried their sob, the pain and relief an excruciating mix. Every door and window called to them, to their weak legs and trembling lungs: get out, get out now, whatever the risk. But they had chosen to trust Maddy. And they would. Damn them both, Diego would trust him.

The rest of the hunters were not so content to have a free vampire, even if *free* was such a relative term for Diego in that moment.

"You're letting them—"

"What the hell, Maddox?"

"I thought you were a *hunter*."

Maddy didn't seem the least bit phased. He shrugged and ran his hand roughly through Diego's hair, gripping it with a tug. "Every now and then I can make an exception, if they're pretty enough and can learn to obey." He let Diego go, and they bowed their head lower, repeating to themself, *starlight, starlight*, as Maddy circled around them. With each predatory pace, the others scooted back from Diego. He grinned. "Tell me you haven't thought about it? Of *keeping* one."

A few of the people in the group—a gathering made primarily of white men, Diego didn't fail to notice— glanced at each other like they most certainly had. One of them squatted, as if he might see into Diego's mouth from the distance. "But you left the fangs in? That's dangerous—dangerous for everyone."

"I told you, they're tame as can be." Maddy nudged Diego's side with his boot, and the laugh he gave would have been chilling if it didn't remind Diego of years of theater practice, every time they'd rolled their eyes and told him there was no way that would fool the audience into thinking he was anything but a DC villain. He'd perfected the smirk along with it, a cruel thing that held all its joy close to the teeth, like happiness could be found only in aggression. "How else am I supposed to get their venom on demand?"

Oh, venom. Diego's stomach dropped, but they could see what he was going for: the inversion of an act that had been played out by others at the club over the last two weeks. They could force themself through it if they had to. For Maddy. To get out of this, and ask him what the fuck he'd been doing here. He had better pray he had a good reason.

The hunters had clearly never seen a vampire and human couple enjoying power play before, their faces shifting between disgust and something like disgusted intrigue. "You let the creature *feed* on you?"

Maddy snorted, coming to a stop in front of one of the tables, where lay a map of the local area and a couple of beer bottles. "Fuck no! No vampire is worthy of *my* blood."

The emphasis was elsewhere, but Diego still caught

the word—worthy—like their own secret code. All they could think of was his wrist slit open, his blood in their mouth, his sounds of pain and pleasure as he gave to Diego without asking for anything in return. It was such the opposite of this sadistic presentation; and they had to believe the person who'd been offering himself up at their feet had been the real one. That man had been their Maddy, and he was still there, underneath the act, taking care of them as always.

"We don't *exchange* anything with them, do we?" Maddy spread his arms, as if Diego, the warehouse, the world, all belonged to him. "*No.* We only take." He snapped his fingers in front of him like he was calling a dog.

Diego went, half stumbling, half crawling, settling onto their knees before him. Their whole body shuddered, the ache in their bones from the sun-poisoning intensified by the movement. They bowed their head, trying just to breathe through it.

Maddy laughed. He withdrew the knife from his belt—a deadly looking thing, long and thick with a dark red, nearly black, caught in the grooves of the hilt. Vampire blood. Diego shuddered again, all horror this time. He lowered the tip of the knife towards them. Their doubts returned: his hand around the pliers, the malevolence in his laugh.

But then he slipped the end of the blade beneath

their chin and delicately tipped it up.

Even in this place, standing between life and death, Diego felt the beauty in the motion, the thrill of staring up the length of a blade into the face of someone who could have easily shoved the tip in but had chosen to stay their hand instead. Maddy turned the knife, not pressing in enough to cut, just following the path where a little scar now sat at the right edge of his own chin, marking the place Diego had cut him the first night he'd barged into their event. His eyes laughed.

This time the shiver that ran through Diego wasn't the least bit distressing.

Maddy pulled the blade away, and they let him press open their lips, eyes only on him as he traced the length of their fangs with a nail. They could have withheld their venom easily, but they let it pool, let him see it glinting, as though to say *this is safe, my starlight; I agree to it.* When he pricked the pad of his thumb, the blissful expression on his face was genuine. The scent of his blood flooded Diego's senses, and they fought the instinct to close their lips and suck. They let Maddy pull his thumb back, let him wipe his pointer finger over their tongue to catch their healing saliva, and watched as he healed the bleeding prick without offering them a drop.

He closed his eyes and smirked, basking like he was settling in a sunbeam, or in the spotlight of a stage. "So long as they're alive, they'll keep making venom for you, so there's always another hit waiting."

It was the first hunter who spoke up, the one who'd cornered Diego in the alley. "Give us a go then, huh? It's not fair if you get some and we don't."

A couple of the others echoed him, and slowly they stepped forward, closing in the gap Maddy's circling had made.

Maddy's expression hardened. He wrapped his fingers through Diego's hair, like by holding them in place he might keep them safe. "I worked hard on this one."

His refusal moved through the gathered hunters, angering them anew. Maddy's breathing shifted, its shallowness the first sign of fear. As much as Diego hated the idea of letting any of the hunters near their fangs, they hated far more the thought that those same hunters might try to rip them away from Maddy and take what they wanted by force. They still weren't sure what Maddy's goal was here, but the longer they knelt beside him, the more signs that it was a performance they picked up on. His act was breaking down. And as much as Diego wanted to see him snatch up the blade once more and turn it on the people surrounding them, they didn't think either of them would come out of that situation alive.

"They're your friends, starlight," Diego murmured,

looking up at him with all the adoration they would never have let shine so brightly if not for the meaning it would impart to him in that moment.

Maddy's throat bobbed. The grip of his hand on their hair slipped for an instant, his thumb rubbing a soft circle. Then he laughed. "I guess even a bat can be right sometimes." He dragged Diego up, rough but steady, both his hands going to their ass. "Let's show them what it's like to have a good time."

Maddy pushed the empty beer cans aside and sat on the table, pulling Diego into his lap. He wrapped an arm around their waist and tugged at their head with his other, pinning the back of their skull to his shoulder. Beneath his show of brutality, his tight grip and solid pressure against their still sun-pained body were like a coddling blanket, a statement that he was there and he would protect them.

Still, it took all of Diego's strength to let their mouth hang open, to put their fangs on display for a group who would have happily ripped them out and displayed them like trophies. Diego let their eyes nearly close, focusing on Maddy's scent and the feeling of his hands on them.

Maddy had bled himself for dozens of vampires in the hopes of bleeding for Diego someday. This was different—different in so many ways—but it was the same too. An act of trust. With every dose of venom they gave up, they tried to ignore the transformation from skepticism and greed to relaxed joy that the hunters experienced. The bastards came away looking so damned pleased that Diego had to force themself not to gag or bite down, thinking instead of the drip of Maddy's blood into cup after cup.

As the last hunter backed away, she gave Diego a longer examination.

"That's one of the vamps from the pervert club, isn't it?" The woman didn't sound accusatory, at least, only thoughtful.

"Yeah. I picked them up while scouting," Maddy said, stealing a final dose of venom for himself.

It was cleansing, somehow, to have him be the last thing in their mouth. Diego loved him for it. They loved him for so many things right then, even if they still hated him for others.

"You think they have more like this bitch?" someone sneered, and the man from the alley echoed the sentiment with a joke crude enough that Maddy stiffened. Diego tipped their forehead against his neck and he seemed to take comfort in their presence the way they had in his, breathing out long and slow.

The woman hunter smiled, as biting as the rest of them. "Guess we'll find out."

"Soon," the alley man put in. "All this sitting around is making me anxious."

Maddy shook his head. "The bloodsuckers aren't

scared enough yet—they're too dangerous. We shouldn't risk our own lives while there's still a chance we can get the authorities to actually do their fucking jobs." He slid Diego off his lap, standing pointedly. One hand came to rest in their hair once more.

"We've warned them again and again by now. If they haven't taken action yet, then it's our responsibility!"

Diego flinched, subconsciously angling toward Maddy. He scoffed, but they could feel the little, gentle circling of his thumb against their scalp. "Still, we can't rush into things."

"We're as ready as we'll ever be," someone protested.

"Send your pet home and let's get this party started," the alley hunter sneered. "It's now or it's never."

And as much as Diego wanted the answer to be never, they had a sinking suspicion that wasn't on the table.

10

The moment Maddox's motorcycle pulled out from the alleyway, Diego was revving on his tail. He lead them in a roundabout loop toward the Celestial Club, screeching to a halt at the club's back door. By the time Diego dismounted, he'd stripped off his helmet and was striding toward them.

They prepared for the worst—for any number of the worsts; dramatic revelations that he hadn't meant to fall back in love with them, that he'd stopped giving the hunters genuine help once he'd realized just how much he cared, that he'd thought one or the other would be a fun diversion and had never intended to get so deep in both worlds. They prepared to rage back, to tell him that he had a lifetime worth of bleeding left to do to make up for this. That if he had helped get them and the club into this mess, he was sure as hell getting them out again.

What they were not prepared for, was Maddox dropping to his knees at their feet, shaking as he pressed his face against their thighs, his palms clutching the back of his head like he was preparing to be cuffed. "I'm sorry. I'm so sorry, Diego."

"What the fuck, Maddy?" They were surprised by just how gentle their own voice had gone. They stroked his hair, drawing his hands off his scalp and pulling his head to their side. When they laced their fingers through his, he hung on for dear life.

"You should never have been subjected to that. I did what I knew would save you; I couldn't think of anything else. But, god, I'm sorry, if I hurt you—"

"Maddy!" Diego gave his hair a little tug, and the jolt seemed to snap him back into place. It snapped the world back into place with it; regardless of what Maddox had done with the hunters previously and the uncomfortable act they'd both had to put on to get Diego out alive, they were still them: a little rough, a lot fierce, but unable to go partway without going all in. "I'm fine. That was horrible—not because of anything you did, but because the hunters were there for it—but I understood. I agreed. And I had you." Maybe the submissive role wasn't their thing, but if they had to submit to anyone, they found they wanted it to be Maddy. "Though if you're going to ask me to play as your pet bat again you're going to have to spill me a *lot* more blood first."

Maddox laughed, soft and wet but relieved. Slowly, he leaned his head against their stomach. "You were incredible, Diego," he whispered. "But I think I prefer being the one on my knees."

"Good." They shoved him just enough to make him wobble. "Because you fucking owe me a lifetime of kneeling. And one very thorough explanation."

He lifted his hands again, palms up this time. "All right, yes, I understand. It's a lot to explain, though. Maybe we should go inside, just to be safe." Maddy sat back on his heels, and he offered Diego both his hands as he stared up at them. "If you trust me enough for that?"

"*Should* I trust you?"

"I have never lied to you, Diego Figueroa."

"Only kept your secrets."

Maddox winced. "I meant it when I said that I wanted you to judge me for who I was. But I owe you the full story." He glanced toward the club's side door.

One of the vampire chefs had poked their head out, and now a second stood with them, looking uncertain. Diego made a shooing motion at them, not because they cared whether other people watched, but because the more audience they had, the more likely there would be interruptions. Diego had waited far too long for this explanation, and maybe that was partially their own fault, but by god, they were getting it.

"Come on, there's probably a spare storage room where you can plead for my forgiveness some more."

They took Maddox's outstretched hands and dragged him up.

He towered over Diego, but when he smiled and bowed his head to them, Diego still felt like *they* were the one on top of the world. "My lord, it would be my honor."

♛

"You know there are two ways this can go." Diego sat on one of the club's unused thrones, one leg slung over its arm and the other propped up, their motorcycle jacket hanging off their knee.

Maddox had chosen a simple bench to perch on, one Diego was pretty sure was meant as a step stool and not a seat at all, but somehow he made it look majestic anyway, like he'd just commenced a war assembly. The stacks of unused cop uniforms Serina had been meaning to cut up threw off the scene a little. Maddox decisively edged his seat away from them.

As he settled again, he exhaled like a man on the executioner's block. "Will I like either outcome?"

"In one of them you bleed for me," Diego explained. "And the other you bleed for me more. So, probably yes." They sighed too, though, running a hand through their own hair and remembering Maddox's grip in it.

Maybe he could do that again, while they bit him, digging their fangs into his flesh until his breath was ragged. "Are you—or were you ever—a hunter?" It seemed like the first, most obvious question.

"Oh, fuck no."

Diego didn't realize how much that possibility had weighed on them until his denial settled in their chest. But then, if he had never been a hunter, why was he working with them?

He must have seen their immediate confusion because he blanched. "I did *play* a hunter in that television show I was in right out of college."

"Red as Blood," Diego said. "Sorry, I looked it up."

Maddox shrugged. "I figured you would. Whether you'll heed anything I beg of you has always been hit and miss." He smiled as he said it, but there was sadness in his eyes too. "I was still half up my own ass when I took that job, but the longer I played the part, the more I hated it—and hated who I'd been and what I'd done to you. I quit as soon as my contract would let me, took all that acting skill and the dramatics of television vampire hunting and found someplace I could put it to better use."

Diego's heart quickened, even though they told themselves it did not matter. So long as Maddox wasn't a hunter, he could be whatever else he wanted. But he *had* hidden this from them, whatever it was. And even now he hesitated. Diego leaned forward, grabbing him by the shirt collar and tugging him forward. "What *kind* of use, Maddy?"

He made a sound, half a laugh and half a sob, and let them draw him off the stool, until he was climbing onto the throne with them, scooping them into his lap and nuzzling against their shoulder. "We're called the Vampire's Liberation Association. We find situations like this, where groups of humans are growing physically aggressive toward the vampires in their neighborhoods, and we do what we can to help."

"Wait—fuck." Diego pulled away enough to stare at him. "You help vampires, for your job. And you didn't want me to know about this? All this time you've had a *get out of jail free* card and you gave me a heart attack keeping it hidden!"

"I'll gladly bleed however much you demand for that." Maddox looked at them like all his blood was already theirs, like it always had been since their eyes first locked the second day of freshman year. "But that's why I didn't want you to know. I didn't want you to take me back just because I was some vampire protector, or because you hoped I could help the club. I needed to know you wanted me not merely for my job but for who I had become."

Diego started to grumble, but then it finally hit them. "Fuck—the club. We have to tell Serina about your work. Maybe they can send someone—"

"Diego," he cut them off, pressing his lips to theirs. "My work sent me. Serina knows. We agreed that for now the best thing was for me to infiltrate the hunters, many of whom already look up to me for the role I played on Red as Blood, then gain their trust as someone with more knowledge and experience, and report back to Serina with their movements."

The reality of it all dawned on Diego slowly, soft and hopeful. "That's what you stayed to talk with her about that first night, why she felt comfortable letting you join our event." He hadn't been there solely for Diego at all. They could hardly hold that against him though. He'd realized they worked at the Celestial Club and done his best to apologize before he'd even spoken with Serina about the club's safety. That was enough. And after all he'd done, they'd still had the nerve to doubt him. "You've been helping us this whole time, and here I thought—" They groaned, fitting their forehead into the crook of his neck. The scent of his blood, dark and dry and oaky, teased their senses. They fiddled with the collar of his shirt, grumbling, "I should probably be pleading for *your* forgiveness."

"No, of course not. You couldn't have known what I'd do if I *was* a hunter after all. I'd have told you much sooner if I'd realized you might be hurt by this." Maddox drew his hand up and down their leg. The sensation tingled beneath their skin, waking them up to just how close their bodies were, how comfortable this had quickly become now that their worry had faded. Maddy pressed his lips to their hair. "Though if you uncover any other seemingly appalling evidence against my morality, ask me about it *before* rushing into a potentially dangerous location, please?"

Diego grabbed Maddox's wrist, shifting his touch from the top of their thigh to the inside. Like the overentitled submissive he'd always been, he took the liberty to press between their legs and teased at the seam of their jeans. The pressure of his fingers left them pleasantly warm and shivery, and they leaned into him, fiddling with the skin above the pulse in his neck. "Do you *have* any other terrible secrets? You should probably come clean now."

"I…" He rolled his shoulders and tipped his chin, like the light scrape and pinch of Diego's fingers was a delightful annoyance. His rubbing increased in force, strong enough to stoke the heat between Diego's legs to a full fire. When he spoke though, he was just as serious as he was desperate. "I never told you this: When you showed me your fangs for the first time, I thought of you biting me—the way it looks in a horror movie, no venom, no bliss, just your pleasure and desire consuming me—and I *wanted* that. It terrified me. I was never as afraid of you as I was of myself."

"Oh." Diego wasn't sure what that knowledge did to them, but their body relished it, venom filling their fangs and a little moan rising in their chest. Or maybe that was just the way Maddox had started moving his fingers. They pressed their lips to the reddened skin they'd agitated atop his pulse. "And now all you have to do is ask."

"Take from me," Maddox whispered. "Take everything."

They sunk their fangs in slowly, savoring the way his body shifted under them, his blood welling between their teeth, warm and delicious. They teased him with their venom, giving a hint for every grunted sound of pleasure his fingers managed to produce from them.

He unzipped their jeans for better leverage, and they rewarded him with a bite deep enough that he flinched and began circling their sensitivity like he was born to make them come. Finally Diego did, slow and long, not quite the peak they'd hit during their night at his apartment, but a more stable, comforting pleasure, half sensation and half knowledge: Maddox belonged to Diego now, their prey and their consort and their savior.

They were going to take so very much more from him and give it all back in equal measure.

They licked and sucked his wound closed with slow, strong intervals, leaving a light bruise on his skin and Maddy himself a moaning puddle beneath them, soft and pliable except for the half-hard form between his legs. They'd help him with that once they felt like standing again. After all Maddy had done for them and their home, all that he'd risked over and over again for vampires he didn't even know simply because they needed someone willing to do so, Diego could happily kneel for him once more.

He deserved that, and so much more.

"You're in a vampire rescue league," Diego marveled. "*You.*" It wasn't shocking, they realized, just thrilling. Of course Maddox wouldn't be a hunter. Of course he'd be a liberator instead.

It made so much sense that it surprised them when he replied, "I've been thinking about leaving, actually." He trailed his fingers up and down their back, his gaze distant and his expression yearning. "I initially joined out of guilt, and I'm proud of what I've accomplished. I've done so much good in these last three years. But then I came here, and I've gotten to experience another type of good that humans can do, the way we can support our vampires not just by dropping in to save the day, but by forging community with them. I've been dancing from job to job, spending more time tearing down the people we're fighting from the inside than building a home for those I've been protecting. I don't just want to be a blade anymore. I want to be a shield, too."

"That..." Diego's throat felt tight suddenly, and they had to force themself to inhale through it, wiping a bit of moisture from their eyes. It took them a moment to place exactly where the emotion was coming from: it was weakness. Not a lack of strength, but the thought of being able to let go. Of *having* a shield. Of being able to breathe, and to breathe deeper, because there was someone standing at their back. "That sounds incredible."

"Does it, truly?" Maddox seemed hopeful, but that optimism shifted to a stoic determination as he sighed, lips pressed to Diego's hair. "Well, it's a dream for tomorrow. Right now the Celestial Club needs a blade, and I'm the only one they've got."

Diego was afraid they were going to need a lot more than that.

♛

They found Serina already discussing the night's progression with Abigail, her scene-creator, and this event's back-stage manager, Adrian, while Valentine patiently took notes.

Maddox pulled Valentine aside first to apologize for the fear he'd inadvertently caused, beaming with affection when Valentine had immediately gone in for a hug. He'd cradled Valentine and kissed the side of his head, and for that one moment Diego didn't think they'd ever been happier. Then Maddox gave Serina a look so serious it zapped all joy from the room. She hurried all five of them back to her office. It was a tight fit, the boarded window making the room claustrophobic. Diego leaned against Maddox, tracing the little raised line that still remained on his wrist as he explained the situation.

Serina wasted no time. "How long do you think we have before the Paladins show up?"

"Twenty-four hours was what they decided," Maddox replied. "They want to burst in as the event is in full swing, take out as many vampires as possible, then light the place up."

Abigail nodded. "That should give us plenty of time to contact everyone, tell them the event is postponed until further notice?"

"And the club itself?" Adrian glanced at Serina, as though validating all the love and attention she'd put into the building's furnishings, from its elaborate set designs and expansive wardrobe to the precisely placed lights that mimicked the stars on the ceiling. "If we're not here, what's stopping them from burning it down?"

Serina looked miserable. "I won't put anyone in danger just to save my business."

"This is more our home than any of the places where

we sleep," Diego objected. "What would we even do without it? We could run small sessions out of people's houses for the money, but that would shatter the community we've built here. We *need* a space that's large enough to gather in, or we're not a community at all, just a bunch of fangs who happen to live in the same city."

Valentine watched Maddox, his eyes dark and his attention unwavering. "Do you think we can get everything out in time?"

Maddy shook his head. "Once we start moving things, they'll notice. I've been keeping close tabs on who's watching this place, and there's enough gaps for me to slip in and out on Juliet, but if we try to move an entire warehouse of stage supplies out, that's going to catch their attention. They won't need to stop us from leaving as long as they can follow to wherever we drive next and transfer their aggression there instead."

The room went quiet, a silence of anxious contemplation as everyone stared into the distance, brows tight. Maddox wrapped his hand around the back of Diego's neck, his long fingers absently feeling the places the holy metal chain had run. Anyone else Diego would have snapped at and shoved off. Even from Maddox, the implication of a collar disquieted them. He seemed to notice, and tugged his hand back, bowing his head to them.

They growled in response. Grabbing his fingers, they lifted his wrist to their lips, kissing it before placing it back on their neck. They would not submit to this—but they could demand it of him instead. This was their narrative too, and like they'd done with the hunters, they could work alongside Maddy to turn it into something good.

With Maddox's steady presence at their side and his fingers tracing their neck once more, they felt the spark of an idea forming. "If we flee with the club's stores, they'll follow wherever we go next. But what if they don't have a reason to hunt us down again?"

"How do we do that?" Valentine asked.

"We give them exactly what they want. They're not just trying to momentarily close the club, they're hoping to put it out of business and then kill or disband the vampires who rely on it. And we can give them that." Diego grinned. "It's what we do, isn't it? Supply people with their fantasies."

The hope that flooded Serina's expression could have set a hunter on fire. "I had better start sewing."

11

The closer they came to setting their plan into motion, the more doubts assaulted Diego. When Maddox left to rejoin the hunters momentarily, their stomach seemed to fall away entirely, leaving a tumbling void beneath their ribs and the taste of bile in the back of their throat. What if this didn't work? What if they didn't have the skill to pull it off?

They had fooled these people once already, Diego reminded themself. The hunters *wanted* what the Celestial Club would be offering them; half the battle was figuring out what that audience would most likely engage with, and these self-proclaimed *Paladins* had been shouting that loud and clear for months. And Maddox had set them up the rest of the way without even realizing it.

"Ready?" Valentine asked.

"Not at all."

He held their crown once more. Today, his part was simple, as was every other vampire who'd volunteered to show their fangs.

All they were expected to do was to risk everything.

It still shocked Diego that Valentine had offered to join in the first place, his face pale and his body twitching with nerves. It looked like it was taking everything in him just to keep himself from retracting his fangs now. But when they'd asked why he didn't go back to the apartment, he'd smiled, soft and sincere despite his fear. *"I'm your right hand. You can't go into battle without me."*

He'd barely left their side for a moment since.

"You don't have any doubts about Maddox?" He didn't sound worried, but rather inquisitive. Knowing him, he was probably gauging whether he needed to offer them emotional support.

Diego thought of every cruel smirk Maddy had given, every cutting utterance of *starlight,* and smiled. "I trust him completely." They had meant to end it at that, but their heart seemed to go on anyway. "Since coming here, this was the only life I'd envisioned. And, fuck, I would have been happy—I would have been so happy just putting on events with you until my hair went grey or my time ran out. But now there's a version of my future where I don't have to *play* the lord. I am one, because I'm his."

They turned toward the warehouse's front doors, where Maddox had just slipped inside. Three vampires jumped to apply the costuming makeup to his neck. He couldn't move his head without accidentally dislodging them, but when his gaze met Diego's with all the intensity of a hurricane, he blinked slow and reverent, his lips twitching up, then turning cheeky as he took in Valentine at their side.

"And *he's* ours," Diego whispered. "Our Maddy."

If he was here, then the hunters would be waiting outside for his return, watching at enough of a distance that those in the club would be safe, but well within view of the demonstration Diego and Maddox planned to conduct at the building's entrance. The final artist finished with Maddox's neck, and Diego strode toward him, they as the king and him, not the consort but the betrayer prince in his leather biker jacket, his knife at his hip and his pocket full of the chains they'd coated with gleaming jewelry paint to mimic his holy silver set. It was time to put on a show. As he extended a hand toward them, though, the front doors rattled.

They burst open.

Diego's heart caught in their throat as hunters streamed through it. They looked so much like a group of B-list actors playing the part that they shouldn't have been so terrifying, but the weapons in their hands were far more deadly than stage props, and the few pieces of holy silver Maddox hadn't managed to swap with replicas burned Diego's exposed skin even with the six feet between them and the nearest sliver of the metal. This was meant to take place on the club's terms—on the club's terms, and *outside*, where no one but Diego would be in immediate danger. They could see their fear echoed in the vampires still preparing around the room. One missed cue and the show was already crashing down.

But Maddox's expression contorted into a domineering sneer, his fingers edging out of his pocket like he was preparing to reveal his holy silver. He held up his free hand, motioning for the hunters to wait by the building's door as he stared down the vampires in the room. "This is your only chance to submit quietly."

The hunters slowed, forming a semi-circle behind Maddox, but their gazes roved over the vampires present and they seemed to waver between fear of the fangs they saw glinting around the room and something almost like hunger. They had all tasted Diego's venom, and some of them had clearly liked the experience, whether for the intoxicant or the dominance or both. In another life, with attitudes less hideous and minds more open, they might have become the very people the club served. Now though, here, they were monsters. And if Diego could not make them suffer for it, at least they could save the Celestial Club to spite them.

"You pathetic bloodsuckers have been taking from humans for too long. Maybe it's time for a change,"

Maddox said, latching onto Diego's shoulder. They could hear the smirk in his voice, so opposite of everything they knew him to be. "You might find you *enjoy* being put in your place."

Diego curled away from his touch, sliding themself into his chest like it was an accident. He yanked them backward, into the midst of the hunters' semi-circle, toward the club's entrance. Each step brought the blaze of the holy silver closer, rekindling the memory of it wrapped about their throat, the certainty that there was no escape. But they settled it beneath the feeling of Maddox's hand, tight and sure on them, his acting so perfect even they couldn't see through it.

"Tell your fanged friends," he growled. "Tell them how you *like* serving me."

"The blonde bat's a pretty little thing," muttered one of the hunters, his attention catching on Valentine. "And he looks about ready to break."

The woman of the group smiled wickedly. "You'll have to catch him before I do."

A visible tremble ran through Valentine, and it seemed to resound in Diego's fresh flood of rage and the anxious tightening of Maddox's grip.

"*Tell* them." He yanked Diego another step back. They were beneath the doorframe now. Almost there. They just needed the hunters to ignore Valentine and follow, if not with their bodies then with their attention.

Diego wheeled on Maddy with a shove that took them both out of the building, pulling everything they had into the motion, emotion and fire and heart-break. Everyone turned to watch, the audience—both those aware and ignorant of the act—drawn naturally to Maddox and Diego's drama, like every audience always had been, since they'd first made it their business that the world knew they'd laid eyes on each other.

"No." Diego didn't shout yet, didn't make it loud or fierce or strong, just a small, scared protest, a choked twist in their voice. "You said you'd give me blood once I—when I'd proved myself."

"I will, as soon as you've *earned* it." Maddox grabbed a fistful of their hair, hard enough that it was barely acting as they whimpered.

They let him push them toward the street, stumbling for the dramatics, and as they faced him once more, they wrapped their arms tight around their stomach, baring their fangs. "When?"

"What." It didn't sound like a question the way he said it, but rather a demand to shut up.

Diego flinched instinctively, and they turned their mind to the memory of Maddox's blood, dripping into cup after cup. "When will I have earned it? When will I be enough for you?" He had always been enough for them, since the moment he knocked on the club's side door, they simply hadn't been able to see it. Yet he had done the impossible and kept proving it to them—was still proving it now, standing before them with a sneer so cruel it made him look like an entirely different person.

"When I say so," he snapped.

Diego glanced back at the club, making a show of their misery, their indecision. The hunters were still watching—all of them, all of them but the woman. She slunk towards Valentine, one of the Paladin's few real pieces of holy silver dangling from her fingers. Valentine stepped back on shaking knees. It was hard to tell from where Diego stood, but they swore his fangs had retracted.

They could feel his terror like it was their own, and their character slipped as a fresh wave of something almost like stage fright tore through their body. They had to be done with this. But it needed to be believable. They lifted their voice, "Give me something now," they begged, "Just a drop. Please."

Maddy glared, fire in his eyes. His fist coiled.

Diego repeated the question louder, stronger, a silent *do it, it's time* hidden beneath the word. "Let me taste you, starlight."

With a crack to the jaw, Maddox knocked them down. The ache of it was bright and hot and Diego wondered for an instant if this was what he felt when he asked for their bite alone, no venom to shield him from the pain. Then they were kneeling, hands on the sidewalk, head ringing. In their peripheral, they could see his fingers beginning to tremble.

Still, his voice remained cold as ice as he growled, "Stay down, or I'll tie you to a cross and burn you up with the building."

He wasted no time, stalking back toward the club. From inside Valentine cried out, a whimpered sound that ravaged Diego's chest. It was now or never. Diego wasn't supposed to be encircled by hunters for this, wasn't supposed to be in danger of vengeance; but they couldn't change that, and they couldn't leave Valentine to suffer for a single moment longer. If it was their life or his, they knew what they'd choose.

The final act had come.

Fangs out and face a mask of rage that was barely a mask at all, Diego launched themselves at Maddox's back. They wrapped one arm around his chest, the other over his shoulder, and tore the tips of their teeth across his neck. The fake skin the stage artists had applied ripped with ease, the bag of real human blood from the club's employee stores pouring out with each pinch of Maddox's arm against it. It filled Diego's mouth as it streamed past their chin and saturated the front of their twinkling suit, dimming the stars one by one. Beneath the unfamiliar blood, Diego tasted something lovely and dark. Fuck—if in their haste they had cut Maddox beneath the fake skin...

But he was already gurgling, struggling, throwing Diego off as he collapsed.

There *was* the scent of his blood underneath, Diego could smell it now, seeping into everything. The hunters were around them, even the woman who'd been going after Valentine, and Maddox was bleeding—really bleeding.

"Starlight..." Maddox muttered, his eyes on them so deep and heavy Diego felt themself dragged into the depth.

Then they closed, and with a shudder, his chest went still.

It was an act. It had to be an act.

But all Diego could sense was his blood now, clogging up their nose and tearing through their chest, and his admission that he would be happy to die at their feet, and the terror tightening like a noose around their chest. They would not lose him. They could not lose their Maddy again. The burn of the hunter's holy silver barely broke them out of their shock, forcing them back—away from Maddox—as a man on their left screamed and lunged for them.

The crackle of a loudspeaker boomed across the street, "Serina Freeman, your establishment is surrounded."

All they wanted was to drop to their knees beside

Maddox, but the world turned to chaos as a group of humans in police uniforms and mock-holy silver bracelets tore out of the dark building across the way.

The loudspeaker continued, "You are under arrest for abetting a dangerous group of homicidal vampires. Everyone on this premises must remain where they are and comply with police authority."

A few hunters turned and fled, but most stood taller, waving the group in blue forward like their vigilante faction had been working with the cops the entire time. From their perspective, perhaps they felt they had—Maddox had certainly told them enough times that this was the best outcome; to get the authorities to step up and do their jobs, rid the city of vampires the way they were supposed to. And here were people with badges and weapons, apparently come to do just that.

Diego forced themself to shy away from the fake holy silver with a hiss as Nina charged them, her red hair tucked back in a low bun. She caught them by the arms, yanking both wrists behind their back. Serina's styling had transformed her from the femme fatale who'd offered herself up as consort two weeks ago to someone barely recognizable. Diego could hear the man next to her giving a crude rendition of rights, but they couldn't drag their gaze from Maddox.

His overwhelming scent filled their lungs and the blue and red lights someone had fitted into their black

SUV flashed against the pooling blood. The silver fox Diego had bitten in place of Maddox the first day he slit his wrist for them was talking to one of the lingering hunters as the rest were guided out of the building, away from the scene of the—alleged—crime.

"We've been keeping tabs on this place for a few weeks now, since a group of concerned citizens tipped us off. We suspect these vampires have been responsible for a lot of local unrest, and it was only a matter of time before one of them showed their true colors again," he explained, serious and congratulatory and just self-righteous enough that even Diego would have bought the act, had they not been the one to run him through the lines four hours ago. "We'll get the others convicted if we dig through their building long enough. That place is a hoard… lots of evidence buried in there."

The last thing Diego saw as they were dragged to the faux undercover police vehicle was someone in a uniform placing a sheet over Maddox's body. He wasn't dead, they reminded themself. This wasn't real, and he wasn't dead.

But they couldn't clear the taste of his blood from their mouth as their car circled around the block and to the safety of an empty parking lot a few streets over. The vehicle that had "arrested" Valentine came around the corner after them, and Diego waved to him as they climbed from their car into the back of the one that would retrieve Maddox.

They hid between the back seats as it started driving, shaking with each bump of the wheels. An eternity seemed to lapse before they came to a stop again. Diego risked peeking out from the side window.

Two humans dressed as EMTs laid a sheet over Maddox and lifted him on a makeshift gurney. No one checked his pulse. Beneath his shroud's red stains, Diego couldn't be sure if there was fresh blood. They didn't know whether it would have been a good sign, or a bad one.

The fake EMTs slid Maddox's gurney into the back of the van, and the doors closed.

Maddox didn't move. But he wouldn't yet—what if a hunter was too near the vehicle, saw him pulling off his old shroud as the car drove around the corner? Diego forced themself to wait the longest ten seconds of their life. The moment they had turned out of sight, they shot over the seats, yanking back the sheet themself.

Maddy still didn't move.

"Maddox! Maddy?"

His eyes stayed closed even as they clutched him to their chest, shouting his name.

Fear as cold as a glacial melt rushed over Diego, tightening their lungs and making their fingers numb.

The wound—they had to close it. If he was still bleeding; was he still bleeding? They couldn't tell. There was so much red on him, so much of his scent choking their mouth and throat, so much of Diego's mind screaming that he was dead, they'd lost him, they'd *killed* him with those very fangs he'd wanted gone a decade ago.

They pressed their tongue to his neck, trying to feel for the cut, or some sign that it was closing. There, was that a shift in the skin? Or just the papery makeup coming off? Fuck, they couldn't tell.

"Maddy!"

He still didn't move.

Blood—he needed blood. Diego couldn't give him that, but they had the second-best thing.

As the car came to a halt three blocks from the club, Diego kissed his neck with their fangs, gently, so gently, pressing their blood-rejuvenating venom into him. The softest sound came from him, something that could have been a moan or could have been his empty lungs settling. Diego gave him their venom again, and again, blessing him with all they'd denied him over the weeks, their stores brimming and their heart wild.

"Come on," they pleaded between bites. "You're my fucking consort, you are not taking your blood away from me again, dammit." The taste of him mixed with salt in their mouth as they sobbed. "Maddy Burke, I fucking love you. Wake up and tell me you love me again, too."

His body made another sound, deeper and uglier. And this time, his fingers twitched in their grip, then tightened around theirs. He mumbled something that sounded a little like, "Did it work?"

Diego laughed and it came out a sob. "You self-destructive shield."

"Sorry." For as weak as his voice was, it held every bit of the intensity and adoration they'd grown to associate with him. "I love you, too. This you." His lashes fluttered, and he met their gaze long enough to smile. "Every damn cell in your body and both your fangs and all your past. I'd like to love your future too, if that's all right."

"You'd better," Diego growled. They turned his face towards theirs and kissed him, and kissed him again, feeding little doses of their venom into him between each press of lips.

He sighed happily, curling against them, but he finally gave their hand a squeeze. "Easy there, with this little blood, too much venom might turn me."

"Fuck, sorry." Diego stopped, then returned to just the kisses, tugging at his lower lip and gripping at his hair. "You have to be human so I can bite you forever."

He curled against them, his trust so complete that it seemed to deepen with every show of control Diego offered, and, eyes closed again, he smiled. "All my blood is yours, Diego."

"How do we have this much *stuff*?" Serina rattled a stack of hats for emphasis, almost knocking down the five at the top. "If we want to set up in a different place every month, we're still going to need a warehouse just to *store* it in."

"You could always split it up," Maddox suggested. He sat in one of the dressing room chairs, still pale and more tired than Diego had ever seen him, but alive. Vampire venom was miraculous, but it was no miracle. Twelve hours was hardly long enough to resupply all the blood he'd lost.

He seemed all right though, otherwise, and of those who'd acted in their con to save the pieces that made the Celestial Club what it was, he had sustained the worst of the physical injuries by far. Valentine still refused to let his fangs back out, and Diego had left him at their apartment wrapped in a blanket with a mug of cocoa spiked with blood—*not* Maddy's, though he'd offered. Maddox had stayed with them both through the day, Diego emerging from the shower to find Valentine curled up against Maddox's side. Maddy had kissed his head before they'd left.

When Diego asked about it, he'd shrugged. "He's a

sweetheart."

Diego gave Maddy a soft shove. "But not *your* sweetheart."

"If he was, would you be jealous?"

Smirking, Diego snatched his wrist and ran their thumb over the thin scar line that remained there. "Why should I be jealous of people who are both already mine?" They laced their fingers with his. "Anyway, Valentine is just a bundle of snuggles, and you have two sides for small vampires to curl up in."

"And two wrists?"

"You will spill your blood for whoever I tell you to."

Maddox smiled, the fire in his gaze so hot it could have been the sun, warm and brilliant and beautiful. "As you wish."

The world had seemed so bright for that moment, but standing in the Celestial Club now, it was clear there would still be hard work ahead of them. Hard work, but worth the effort, even if Diego hated that it had to be done in the first place. This warehouse had been beautiful, and while they were sure to recreate that beauty again, turning the club into a mobile secret felt like a step back instead of forward. They would still set up in large spaces, still cater to the same size crowd, but by shifting location with every new event, Serina hoped they could avoid situations like the one the Paladins had put them in.

Finding places to move between would never have been possible if not for Maddox connecting Serina with his Vampire's Liberation contacts throughout the city. Without him, the whole place would no longer exist. Without him...

Diego had spent ten years without him, and they wouldn't endure another minute.

Maddy hummed thoughtfully, his gaze sweeping the dressing room like he was giving the space life just by looking at it. "You know, San Salud could use a place like the Celestial Club, and I bet my family has an old warehouse we could spare."

Serina huffed. "I'm not leaving LA for your cemetery town, no offense. A *lake* is not a *beach*."

"I wouldn't dream of asking you to," Maddox said with a laugh. He turned solemn though, and he seemed to struggle over his words, like he was... nervous? "But Diego and I, we could reach more vampires if *we* went there, ran a second set of events." He glanced toward Diego, and added, quickly, "That is, if he wanted to help me in that."

He, Diego—Maddox's lover. Maddox's *boyfriend*.

Maddy looked at Diego, finally, a tiny, hopeful quirk in his lips. "*Does* he want to?"

"He thinks it sounds terrifying and impossible and absolutely outrageous," Diego replied, and grinned. "So why not?" They tossed a spare hat at Serina, nearly knocking down the stack of them she stood beside. "But you'll teach us, won't you, Serina?"

"What the hell am I supposed to teach *you*, Diego? You know my business better than I do by now." Serina smiled. "But I'll always be here if you need help. And you have to take Valentine. He'll turn into a sad puppy if you leave him here alone."

"As though we'd ever abandon him." Diego snorted. "We're not running away either. If we're doing this, we're doing it to *grow* the Celestial Club." They came up behind Maddox as they said it, running their hand through his hair with the rough grip he always swooned under. "We're not losing our family, or our home, no matter how much the Paladins wanted to take it from us. We're just making it bigger."

Maddy leaned into their touch, the joy and comfort on his face seeming so contrary to the way Diego tugged, yet perfect all the same. "What should we call it?" he asked.

"Something like Starlight, I think."

"Something like Starlight," Maddox repeated.

12

Epilogue

The first thing they saw as they came over the final hill was the night skyline against the lake. San Salud was one of the few places that was always more gorgeous at night, like it had been built knowing its excess of cemeteries would someday make it a hub for ghost tours. And vampires.

Maddox had already reached out to his fanged friends in the city. The people who'd been in Diego's life when he'd last lived there might have abandoned him, but he'd have a new home, a new family. The three of them would make one, out of the supplies in the trailer behind their truck and their determination and love. Together, they would build something great, and Maddox would be his vampire's sword and shield every step of the way.

As though Diego knew Maddox's thoughts, his boyfriend's hand slipped across the truck's center console and wrapped around Maddox's. Maddox glanced at him, one long look that made his heart swell. Ten years had been far too long, but somehow it had still brought them here. Brought them home again, better and stronger and surer than they'd ever been.

They'd make up for the lost time with every year to come: the prince and his lord, and everyone who loved them.

Diego, Maddox, and Valentine (along with the new club they create) will return in the third novel of the *Guides for Dating Vampires* series!

Until then, check out books one and two for more steamy achillean vampire romance with healthy relationships that bite, or sign up for D.N. Bryn's newsletter for post-book scenes of spicy and fluff as Diego's polycule lives their best lives!

CHECK OUT THE REST OF THE *BOUND BY BLOOD* SERIES FOR MORE SPICY VAMPIRE ROMANCES!

The Sacrifice and the Spare, an MF arranged marriage romance by Elle Backenstoe

The Tainted and the Tamed, an MF slow-burn, class different romance by C.K. Beggan

The Hawk and the Nightingale, an MF forbidden love romance by Jennifer Allis Provost

The Magnolia and the Bleeding Heart, an FFF second chance mafia romance by River Bennet

The Nettle and the Nightmare, an FFM enemies-to-lovers romance by Alora Black

The Thorn and the Thistle, an MF forbidden romance by Kendra Corbeau

The Moon and the Hunt, an MF fated mates second chance romance by Ophelia Wells Langley

Content in this book includes:

An extensive scene of **sexual intimacy** in which one partner eagerly consents to experiencing **pain** in the form of being bitten by a vampire's fangs.

Multiple scenes where a character consensually **slits a vein** in his wrist to bloodlet for a vampire.

One scene in which a character implies they might **slit a vein** in their neck for vampire-feeding purposes (is not followed through on).

Talk of a past **major depressive episode**, including **suicidal ideation** during that time.

Minor **PTSD-like symptoms** that resolve quickly.

References to the **police**, including mentions of real world police violence and the police's high likelihood of harming the marginalized communities they are meant to protect.

Made in the USA
Columbia, SC
15 September 2023